IS IT WRONG TO TRY TO PICK UP GIRLS IN A DUNGEON?
MINOR MYTHS AND LEGENDS
2

© nilitsu

Contents

Sword Oratoria Volume 1 —— iv

Sword Oratoria Volume 2 —— 018

Sword Oratoria Volume 3 —— 028

Sword Oratoria Volume 4 —— 056

Sword Oratoria Volume 5 —— 066

Sword Oratoria Volume 6 —— 076

Sword Oratoria Volume 7 —— 086

Sword Oratoria Volume 8 —— 112

Sword Oratoria Volume 9 —— 122

Sword Oratoria Volume 10 —— 132

Sword Oratoria Volume 11 —— 136

Sword Oratoria Volume 12 —— 140

Familia Chronicle Episode Lyu —— 150

Familia Chronicle Episode Freya —— 158

Miscellaneous —— 170

Bonus Short Story —— 212

MINOR MYTHS AND LEGENDS

2

FUJINO OMORI

ILLUSTRATION BY
nilitsu

CHARACTER DESIGN BY
SUZUHITO YASUDA

New York

IS IT WRONG TO TRY TO PICK UP GIRLS IN A DUNGEON?
MINOR MYTHS AND LEGENDS, Volume 2
FUJINO OMORI

Translation by Jake Humphrey
Cover art by nilitsu

This book is a work of fiction. Names, characters, places, and incidents are the product of the author's imagination or are used fictitiously. Any resemblance to actual events, locales, or persons, living or dead, is coincidental.

DUNGEON NI DEAI WO MOTOMERU NO WA MACHIGATTEIRUDAROUKA SHOHENSHU, vol. 2
Copyright © 2023 Fujino Omori
Illustrations copyright © 2023 nilitsu / Suzuhito Yasuda
All rights reserved.
Original Japanese edition published in 2023 by SB Creative Corp.
This English edition is published by arrangement with SB Creative Corp., Tokyo in care of Tuttle-Mori Agency, Inc., Tokyo.

English translation © 2025 by Yen Press, LLC

Yen Press, LLC supports the right to free expression and the value of copyright. The purpose of copyright is to encourage writers and artists to produce the creative works that enrich our culture.

The scanning, uploading, and distribution of this book without permission is a theft of the author's intellectual property. If you would like permission to use material from the book (other than for review purposes), please contact the publisher. Thank you for your support of the author's rights.

Yen On
150 West 30th Street, 6th Floor
New York, NY 10001

Visit us at yenpress.com · facebook.com/yenpress · twitter.com/yenpress
yenpress.tumblr.com · instagram.com/yenpress

First Yen On Edition: June 2025
Edited by Yen On Editorial: Ivan Liang
Designed by Yen Press Design: Andy Swist

Yen On is an imprint of Yen Press, LLC.
The Yen On name and logo are trademarks of Yen Press, LLC.

The publisher is not responsible for websites (or their content) that are not owned by the publisher.

Library of Congress Cataloging-in-Publication Data
Names: Ōmori, Fujino, author. | nilitsu, illustrator. | Humphrey, Jake, translator.
Title: Is it wrong to try to pick up girls in a dungeon? minor myths and legends / Fujino Omori ; illustrations by nilitsu ; translation by Jake Humphrey.
Other titles: Danjon ni deai wo motomeru no wa machigatteirudarouka souhenshuu. English
Description: First Yen On edition. | New York : Yen On, 2025– | Audience term: Teenagers
Identifiers: LCCN 2024054622 | ISBN 9798855410983 (v. 1 ; trade paperback) | ISBN 9798855411003 (v. 2 ; trade paperback)
Subjects: CYAC: Short stories. | Fantasy. | Adventure and adventurers—Fiction. | LCGFT: Fantasy fiction. | Action and adventure fiction. | Short stories. | Light novels.
Classification: LCC PZ7.1.O54 Ise 2025 | DDC [Fic]—dc23
LC record available at https://lccn.loc.gov/2024054622

ISBNs: 979-8-8554-1100-3 (paperback)
979-8-8554-1101-0 (ebook)

10 9 8 7 6 5 4 3 2 1

LSC-C

Printed in the United States of America

Minor Myths and Legends

— (2) —

DRESS-UP AIZ

It all started five years ago, when Aiz Wallenstein was eleven years old.

"Aiz, your clothes are gettin' a bit small, ain't they? Why don'tcha change into these?"

In those days, Aiz was just beginning to come into her own as an upper-class adventurer, and her equipment consisted of sturdy, leather undergarments topped with armor, including her metal breastplate. Loki's keen eye quickly spotted that the child's chest and hip areas, in particular, were growing, and her equipment was becoming a little too tight to accommodate her blossoming growth.

"...Aren't these a bit thin...?" asked Aiz as she took the clothes Loki offered and examined them. "They should be leather..."

"Oh, no, these are specially made, li'l Aiz! They're as strong as anything, but they'll grow with you and let you move as smooth as butter!"

Loki's sheer enthusiasm left the young Aiz little choice but to accept. Sure enough, the garments felt stretchy and light, just as Loki had promised. So long as Aiz had something more protective to wear on top, she didn't see an issue with them.

"I also got you this skirt. What's that? Worried everyone'll see your knickers? Just wear spats, and that won't be a problem!"

After that, Loki bought many new outfits for Aiz, insisting each was the latest development in armor technology.

"These are thigh-high boots. You absolutely gotta wear these! That's why they call it 'Absolute Territory'!"

While the quality steadily increased with each new offering, the quantity of fabric seemed to do the exact opposite.

"Erm…isn't this a bit much?"

"Never! You gotta wear this, Aiz! If you don't put it on, I'll kill myself!"

Before long, Aiz was wearing clothes that would make an Amazon blush.

"Heh-heh-heh, now ain't that a sight for sore eyes? If only all adventurers dressed like this…"

"…"

And in the present day, Aiz's battle clothes were little more than a leotard. She had long since grown used to Loki's leering gaze by now, but that didn't stop her whole body from burning with embarrassment whenever those eyes fell on her exposed armpits or the gentle curve of her back.

"Huh-huh-huh. Actually, Aiz, I've already planned your next outfit," said the goddess with glee as she admired the girl's rosy cheeks.

"…What is it this time?"

The corners of Loki's lips curled upward.

"A bunny suit!"

The next day, Loki was found beaten to a pulp in the center of the courtyard.

MEOWNE

"Meow!"
"…"

Finn could only offer an awkward silence. Crouched on the desk before his very eyes was his junior, Tione. A pair of false ears jutted out from her head like a catgirl's, while an equally feline tail extended from her shapely hindquarters, seemingly attached via a novelty headband and undergarment.

Finn had been researching alone in the home library when the door silently opened, and in came Tione, complete with cat ears and all. She then proceeded to climb onto the table, raise one hand like a paw, and executed what could only be described as a premeditated attack on Finn's psyche.

"…What are you up to, Tione?"

"Well, Loki said if you do this, then any man will fall into your arms! Heh-heh-heh…I thought maybe I'd try it on you, Captain…"

While Finn began devising an appropriate punishment for his mischievous patron goddess, Tione squeezed her arms together, pushed her breasts up, and gazed lovingly into Finn's eyes. The prum commander responded by drawing his chair a little farther down the table, in the opposite direction.

"What do you think, Captain…? Does it make your heart skip a beat?"

"It makes my skin crawl"—was what Finn wanted to answer, but he valiantly resisted. Tione looked like a pussycat, but make no mistake—this was a vicious lioness, eager to pounce on her prey if given half a chance. It was important to placate her without overstimulating her, so Finn gingerly extended an arm and stroked Tione's head softly.

"Eh-heh-heh," giggled the Amazon, fidgeting shyly beneath his touch. "I got you one, too, Captain. Meow we can match!"

Tione swiftly plonked a second set of cat ears atop her captain's head. Where had they come from, exactly…?

"C-Captain…! It's too cute! I can't take it…! I want to gobble you up right!"

She's going into heat!

Watching the predator's cheeks flush scarlet, Finn feared for his well-being and dashed out of the room like a rabbit on the run. And hot on his heels was a king of beasts, more terrifying than any monster the Dungeon could produce.

And, man and woman alike, everyone who caught sight of the cat-eared Finn running across the courtyard felt a burning urge to reaffirm their familial loyalty.

MISBEGOTTEN UNION

Lefiya confronted Tiona when the two were alone in the *Loki Familia* common room.

"E-erm, Ms. Tiona! I think you're clinging to Ms. Aiz far too much without good reason!"

"Hmm? Am I?" Tiona responded lazily from the sofa.

"Y-yes you are!" yelled Lefiya. "You'll use almost any excuse to hug her all the time!"

It had been on Lefiya's mind for a while now. It wasn't like the elf girl was jealous or anything; she was just…concerned. *Somebody* needed to teach Tiona the proper way to behave in public…or at least that was the rationalization Lefiya used to convince herself.

"You know what they say: A hedge between keeps friendships green."

"Yeah, but Aiz and I are *best* friends, so it's okay," Tiona replied, without overthinking it.

Lefiya gnashed her teeth and growled, unable to respond.

"If you're so mad about it, why don't you hug her, too?"

"Wh-where did that come from?!" Lefiya shrieked, taking several swift steps in retreat as the tips of her ears turned bright red.

Tiona nonchalantly hopped to her feet and spread her arms. "Let's practice," she said. "Pretend I'm Aiz and come at me with all you've got!"

"M-Ms. Tiona?! What are you saying?!"

Tiona simply smiled, urging Lefiya to overcome her shyness.

"Aiz is really soft and warm, you know."

Lefiya gulped. An untoward thought crossed her mind: *If I hug Tiona, wouldn't that sort of be like hugging Aiz as well?!*

And so, after a long pause, Lefiya cast aside her doubts and threw herself into the Amazon's arms.

"Oh, Aiz."

"?!"

Just then, right as their bodies came together, the woman of the hour entered the room and froze upon seeing such an unexpected scene.

"...I'm sorry. I'll come back later."

"Waaait! Ms. Aiz! I can explaaaain!!"

CHASING UNICORNS

"Mwa-ha-ha-ha-ha! Loki! I got a quest for you!!"

"What's this fool snickerin' about...?"

It was a bright, sunny afternoon in the *Loki Familia* household, and Aiz and the rest of the gang had been relaxing all day when a visitor arrived—Dian Cecht, accompanied by his follower, the silver-haired healer Amid.

"Your familia scammed quite a hefty sum out of mine the other day, so I'm here to pay back the favor!" the old man growled. "You wouldn't turn down another quest, now, would you?! Mwa-ha-ha-ha-ha!"

Aiz, Tiona, Lefiya, and Loki gathered in the front garden inside the gates to receive Dian Cecht and Amid. They each turned to Tione—the instigator of this mess—and shot her a deadly glare.

"...Tione."

"Wh-what?! I didn't do anything wrong!"

"...Well, let's hear it, then, old man. I ain't sayin' we'll accept, but whatcha got?"

"Hah! Very well! Amid!"

The two gods sat down at a white table while Amid stepped forward. "Recently, a unicorn has been spotted on the outskirts of Orario," she began.

Aiz and the other girls were stunned, while Loki, hands clasped behind her head, raised a single eyelid.

Unicorns were a kind of monster, but they were treated more like divine beasts, with beautiful, snow-white coats and a single prized horn. They were counted among the most elusive denizens of the Dungeon, and many upper-class adventurers went their whole lives without seeing one. And of course, locating a unicorn aboveground was a virtually impossible task.

"Several of the city's adventurers are hunting down this rare monster as we speak. It hardly bears mentioning what they all seek: the horn. We at *Dian Cecht Familia* would also like to procure this item for our own purposes."

The horn of a unicorn was said to possess the ability to neutralize any poison. For a group specialized in healing like *Dian Cecht Familia*, it was a highly coveted item, and even disregarding that, the horn itself fetched an exorbitant price on the market.

"If possible, we would also like to return the unicorn to its habitat alive," Amid went on.

"…It can't ever be simple, can it?" remarked Tione with a sigh.

After seeking a new life on the surface, the unicorns had apparently started a new herd deep in the sacred mountains, and Amid very much wished to avoid seeing this fledgling species wiped out.

The proposed quest was shaping up to be a troublesome one, but just as the upper-class adventurers exchanged worried glances, Loki spoke up.

"Sounds fun. Consider me interested."

Horrified gazes converged on their bigmouthed leader, yet Loki ignored them and went straight to negotiations.

"So what's in it for us? Do we get a piece of this pie you're cookin'?"

"Indeed. Should you succeed in obtaining the horn of the unicorn, we shall apportion a share of the material to you."

"Woohoo! Sounds good to me! Count us in!"

"Hey, wait!"

"Lokiii!"

Loki, something of an aficionado for rare items herself, was quickly consumed by the prospect of adding another to her collection. Tione and Tiona were annoyed she hadn't consulted them, or any members of the familia, before accepting the proposal, but the goddess wore the boots around here, and that was just how it worked.

Dian Cecht hollered with laughter. "Mwa-ha-ha-ha-ha! That's settled, then!"

"So how we gonna do this?" Loki inquired. "Ain't nobody ever captured a unicorn alive before."

"It is said that unicorns are attracted to those pure of heart," Amid explained. "We must exploit that fact."

"'Pure of heart,' ya say? So we gotta put together a party of virgins?"

"'V-virgins'…?!" repeated Lefiya, her face going bright scarlet.

One old legend claimed that after coming to the surface, a herd of unicorns played with a beautiful spirit girl deep in the forest and formed a connection with her. It was said that ever since then, unicorns were attracted to the pure and chaste—which, in the case of mortals, meant an unspoiled virgin—and could easily be charmed to fall asleep in their arms. Whether or not the legend was true, unicorns did seem to behave this way by all accounts.

"Then these four girls should do the trick," said Loki. "They might be virgins, but they're a darn sight more terrifying than any unicorn."

"And I'll send my Amid to aid you!" the old god added.

Left out of negotiations as usual, the familia members themselves breathed a collective sigh of dismay.

And so it was decided that the quest for the unicorn would go ahead. As thoughts shifted from the futile task of railing against their fate and toward notions of how it would be done, Lefiya asked her Amazonian associates a question.

"Erm, Ms. Tione, Ms. Tiona? Are you sure you have the necessary…ahem…prerequisites?"

Her cheeks flushed, making Lefiya's preconceived notions of the Amazon race perfectly clear. Luckily, the two sisters didn't seem to take offense.

"I am saving myself for the captain," replied Tione with apparent pride.

"I've never done it with any boys or anything," said Tiona simply.

"I-I see," said Lefiya, still blushing.

"Amid's my personal assistant," said Dian Cecht, "and there's a mountain of work waiting for her back at home. Which means I have to put a time limit on this quest: three days! Mwa-ha-ha-ha-ha!"

"Three days…"

Aiz thought of how she could better use that time training or delving deep into the Dungeon, but Tiona noticed her despondent look and hugged her from behind.

"You have to come with us, Aiz!" she said cheerily.

Loki also gave a crafty grin. "Don't think you're wriggling your way outta this one, Aiz."

"…"

And so Aiz was forced to participate as well.

The unicorn sightings mostly centered around a grassy region bordering on the forest at the base of the Beor Mountains, due north of Orario.

It was the day after *Loki Familia* accepted Dian Cecht's quest. The previous day had been mostly taken up by paperwork with the Guild—even though the old god had already arranged many things in advance—so it was only now that Aiz and the rest of her unit sallied forth from the north gate, with Amid accompanying them.

"So hey, Amid. How come we can't just throw a net over it or something?"

"Unicorns are noble creatures," the healer replied. "If one is trapped, they will rage madly and could very well end up taking their own life."

Word had apparently gotten around regarding *Loki Familia*'s interest in the unicorn, because the group found their path barred at every turn by adventurers—hunters seeking the beast's materials for themselves. However, none of them could slow the team down for very long. Some of the girls even took it upon themselves to flush out the poachers personally, reasoning that the hunters' very presence jeopardized the mission—which arguably stretched the definition of self-defense.

After wiping out most of the hunters, the group picked up the unicorn's tracks and followed them into the highlands. As the party crested a hill, Lefiya raised a finger and pointed.

"L-look over there!"

When the others saw what she saw, it took their breath away.

A beautiful coat of white fur, like freshly fallen snow, spanned all the way up its supple legs to the tip of its tail. The single horn sprouting from the crown of its noble head boasted a spiral groove that ran to the tip. Seeing it dash across the plains made it easy to understand why people considered it a divine animal.

The unicorn.

"Wow! I've never seen one before!" exclaimed Tiona.

"It's so beautiful," muttered Tione. "It's hard to believe it's a monster."

Even the taciturn Aiz widened her eyes at the sight and continued watching the beast for some time.

Upon closer examination, the beast's white fur was streaked with flecks of blood, and it had clearly met with some hardship at the hands of hunters and their traps. From time to time, it would raise its head and scan the plain, wary of further danger. Aiz and her party observed the beast from a low hill, lying flat on their stomachs so as not to alarm it, while they devised a plan of attack.

"Who's going first, then?" asked Tiona.

"Hm? Aren't we all going?" replied Lefiya.

"We can't do that! If we all go at once, it'll be too overwhelmed by purity to know who to pick!"

"...I'm not so sure about that," Amid interjected, "but we may well scare it off. Perhaps Tiona has the right idea; we should send a couple of us and see how things go."

At Amid's wise words, the whole group agreed. Tiona eagerly volunteered to be the first test subject, while dragging her reluctant sister along for the ride.

"...So we're up first...?"

"Let's make it a game, Sis: Who can charm the unicorn first, you or me?"

The other girls stayed back on the hill for moral support while the twins approached the animal.

"Now that I think about it, how do we even charm a unicorn?" asked Tione.

"That's obvious!" squealed Tiona as she pranced ahead, leaving her sister behind. "Just pretend it's a doggy! Good boy! Come here!"

Her sudden appearance startled the beast, but Tiona paid it no heed, spreading her arms and smiling, while beckoning it over. The unicorn studied the girl with eyes like sapphire gems, then seemingly lost interest and turned away.

"I thought for sure that would work..." Tiona moaned. Her elder sister sighed and decided to try for herself.

Taking care not to appear threatening, Tione softly approached the animal. Once at a safe but amicable distance, she pondered how best to proceed before finally breaking the ice with an awkward smile.

The unicorn barely registered her presence before swiftly turning its back.

"Ah-ha-ha-ha-ha!" Tiona burst into uproarious laughter. "Look at that! It didn't care!"

"That's basically the same way it treated you!!" Tione angrily protested.

Defeated, the two Hyrute sisters returned to the hill to the consolation of their peers. Next up was Lefiya. She timidly approached, and it looked as if the elf girl might succeed, but as soon as she extended an arm to stroke the beast, the unicorn whinnied and stepped away.

"Eep!"

The girls on the hill emitted disappointed groans as Lefiya trudged dejectedly back to base.

"This is one fussy pony," said Tiona. "It hasn't given us a chance at all!"

"It's not easy training a monster," reasoned Tione. "That's why tamers have such difficult jobs."

"This might take longer than I thought…" said Amid, turning to Aiz with a somewhat apologetic look. "Do you want to try next, Aiz, or shall I?"

"…I'll give it a go."

Backed by Tiona's cheers of encouragement, Aiz stepped down the hill. The unicorn was idly munching grass in the center of the beautiful, green field when its head jerked up at her approach. Staring into the blond-haired girl's golden eyes, it turned its body and lowered its horn.

Ah, it's scared.

It's definitely scared.

It's so scared…

The creature is frightened.

The four girls on the hill shared similar thoughts. They could almost feel the tension in the air as the unicorn fought valiantly to steady its trembling knees.

Aiz trudged back droopy shouldered, and so Amid was the last to make an attempt.

"…"

Upon reaching the edge of the field where the unicorn was grazing, Amid got an idea and sat down in place. Seated on the grass, she stared over and caught the unicorn's gaze. When the beast saw this fair-faced, fair-hearted maiden, it took a few uncertain steps before slowly beginning to approach. Everyone on the hill leaned forward in amazement as the white animal settled beside Amid, folded its legs, and laid its large head in her lap.

There under the blue sky, a single unicorn took a gentle repose—a beast of legend and a beautiful maiden at ease in a vast meadow, just like a masterpiece painting from a child's fairy tale.

Then Amid's hand went to her waist as she withdrew the knife hidden within the folds of her robe. While the beast rested with its eyes closed, she gingerly brought the blade closer and closer to the coveted horn. Just as it was about to reach, the unicorn's eyes shot open, and it sprang to its feet, throwing Amid aside before scampering off.

"Amid!" the girls cried, rushing down the hill. "Are you okay?!"

"I-I'm fine, just a little shaken, that's all..."

Amid glanced at her knife, flung aside in the chaos, and cast repentant eyes after the unicorn.

"It appears that its experience with the hunters has left this animal rather scarred," she said. "It seems...excessively afraid of people."

The group glanced toward the unicorn, which had put a great distance between itself and the girls. It gave one last betrayed whinny, then turned and ran away. Tiona, Tione, and Lefiya made defeated faces, while Aiz helped Amid to her feet before turning to stare after the retreating beast.

The group found no luck following the unicorn's trail that afternoon and spent the entire following day searching in vain. At last, the final day of their imposed time limit arrived.

Brimming with vigor and resolve, the girls headed deep into the forest, following the animal's trail into the thick foliage at the base of the Beor Mountains.

"Even if we find it," said Tiona, "do you really think the unicorn is gonna give us another chance? I'm not sure we can take its horn without doing something dramatic. What do you think, Amid?"

"...You may be right."

Keeping the unicorn alive was Amid's personal preference and not part of the quest. It was beginning to look as if the healer girl might be forced to set aside her own feelings for the sake of the mission, and the guilt on her face made it clear that the decision was not an easy one.

Before long, the party came upon the unicorn once more, nestled in a clearing beside a cool stream. The creature noticed the girls approaching and watched them warily, leaving them unsure how to proceed.

Suddenly, they heard a voice.

"...I found you."

"L-Lady Riveria?!"

Lefiya exclaimed in shock as Riveria appeared behind them on horseback. She smoothly dismounted her steed and joined the five girls.

"Riveria," said Aiz. "Why are you here?"

"Loki sent me," the high elf responded with mild annoyance. "She said to assist you and ensure the successful completion of your quest."

It transpired that Loki hadn't briefed Riveria on what the quest actually was, so Amid explained, and by the end, the high elf seemed taken aback. "Oh, is that all?" she said and began walking over toward the unicorn.

"R-Riveria?" exclaimed Tiona.

At first, the beast was wary, but when it looked into Riveria's jade-green eyes, it seemed to immediately relax, allowing her to come closer. As the girls watched in total shock, Riveria cradled the animal's head and brought it to her own cheek.

"We had one of these beautiful creatures back in the high-elf village," she said as if it was nothing. "I know how to handle them. Don't worry."

The girls watched, unable to believe their eyes or ears, as Riveria stroked the beast's large neck.

"These are a lot friendlier than the brutish monsters you find in the Dungeon," she added.

Before long, the unicorn was completely at ease in Riveria's arms. "Is Lady Riveria perhaps some kind of master tamer…?" muttered Lefiya.

"I'm sorry," said Riveria to the animal, "but could you share your horn with us? We swear we shall not use it for evil."

To everyone's surprise, Riveria made no attempt to steal the unicorn's horn. Instead, she beseeched the beast to give it freely. The creature brayed softly in response before lowering its head in offering.

"A knife, please," said Riveria, and Amid panicked before stepping forward with a blade.

Meticulous yet gentle, Riveria removed the horn with astonishing swiftness. The quest was complete.

"I shall guide this one back to its herd," said Riveria as she remounted her horse, borrowed from a merchant in the city. "You girls return home now."

She set off, unicorn in tow, toward the Alv Mountains. The sound of hoofbeats followed her into the depths of the forest.

The five girls stood silently in shock as the woman departed, having completed the quest in their place. A dry wind swept through the trees, and a somber mood descended upon the group. Each of them shared a sorrowful look before turning and heading back to town.

"Hey, Loki, don't you think you could have just sent Riveria in the first place?"

The next day after turning in their quest, Tiona confronted Loki when the two of them were home. It didn't seem fair that five girls had needed to waste three days in pursuit of the unicorn when the high elf could have settled it in a matter of moments.

"Yeah!" agreed Tione.

"Ah, well...you see, I mostly just wanted to see what kinda tomfoolery you'd get up to!"

When the Amazonian twins saw their goddess's smarmy grin, they were livid. Loki beat a swift retreat while the two girls chased after her. Lefiya smiled awkwardly and, along with Aiz, followed the trio out to the entrance hall—just in time to see Loki apprehended.

At that moment, the door to the mansion opened, and a visitor appeared. She looked down at Loki, saw the two Amazonian girls piled on top of her, and tilted her head.

"Am I disturbing something?" she asked.

"Ms. Amid?" said Lefiya, as she and Aiz stepped over the pile on the floor to greet their guest. "Why have you come?"

"As agreed, I've brought the reward for the quest," Amid answered. Then, smiling, she reached into her pocket, pulled out a bundle wrapped in cloth, and handed it over. As Aiz unwrapped it, she and Lefiya were dumbstruck by the sight.

"I made this from the unicorn's horn," Amid explained. "It can turn any poisoned or impotable fluid into clean, drinkable water."

"It's beautiful..." gasped Lefiya.

"Oh, what's this?"

Upon hearing the commotion, Tiona and Tione hopped to their feet and peered into Aiz's palm. Even Loki stood up and tried to squeeze her head through the crowd.

"Ohh! Now that's a real beaut!"

It was a snow-white drinking cup, so beautifully carved and engraved with gold and silver lining that not a trace of the horn's former shape remained. This was the Unicorn's Cup, an item with the power to cleanse any poison. Aiz gazed at it and smiled warmly.

DO AIZ WALLENSTEINS DREAM OF WHITE RABBITS?

Another dream.

Ever since meeting that adventurer boy, Aiz thought, she had been having more and more of them.

This night's dream featured a young Aiz and a rabbit with pure white fur. The rabbit, however, was dressed a little oddly, wearing a yellow waistcoat and carrying a charming, little toy knife. It had big, round scarlet eyes and a pocket watch hanging around its neck, which it frequently observed with great distress, exclaiming "I'm late! I'm late!" while hopping along upright as fast as its two legs would carry it.

The young Aiz was about five years old, and at that age, she was such a terrible rascal that those who knew her today would hardly recognize her. She chased the white rabbit all over and finally managed to catch it in her tiny clutches.

The child, much heartened by her success, let out a cry of delight and hoisted the white rabbit up by its ears, gripping them tightly with both hands. The rabbit dangled helplessly, flailing its little arms and legs in a futile attempt to escape.

Watching this unfold, Aiz was understandably upset. She marched over to her younger self, tapped her hard on the shoulders, and said, "You can't do that!"

The younger Aiz let out a sad whine as Aiz scooped up the white rabbit, holding its soft, fuzzy form in both arms. For a moment, an indescribable happiness washed over her, only to be broken when she finally noticed the expression the rabbit was making.

It was afraid.

Its big, round rubellite eyes quivered in their sockets, and it let out a terrified squeak. Aiz was shocked to have frightened it so, and while she was still taken aback, the white rabbit hopped out of her arms and bolted away.

Aiz stood there, frozen, while her younger self groaned, "Aww, you scared it off…" and shot her a rotten glare. Aiz was so mortified she couldn't move a muscle.

"…A dream."

The morning light shone between the curtains, rousing Aiz from slumber. Her dream had felt so real that she woke up drenched in sweat. She got out of bed and went to take a shower, guilt ridden over what she had seen.

Approximately ten days later, Aiz's dream became reality.

A REASON TO FALL IN LOVE

Six years ago, when Aiz was a full head shorter than she was today, Bete Loga joined *Loki Familia*. Aiz had no idea what circumstances had led to his admission, but the young werewolf's mercenary outlook was evidently the reason he looked down on Aiz from the moment they met.

"Ugh. We really takin' this stinkin' kid with us? Send her back to the nest before the monsters mess up her pretty doll face."

"…"

"Nothin' I hate more than dealin' with useless women and children."

His amber eyes heaped scorn on her from on high, and he always seemed to be in a bad mood. The blue tattoo across his brow wrinkled as he mocked her, even in plain sight of Finn or the other leaders of the familia. He spoke as if he wished she would just disappear.

Of course, even Aiz was not made of stone. She responded with a peeved look, but it was so subtle that only Finn and other veterans noticed. Her first impression of Bete was simple—a bully.

Then she went on her first expedition with him.

"Hey, kid. Get behind me so your shakin' doesn't throw off my game."

After reaching the lower floors without issue, the party ran into a pack of monsters. Bete made his usual snide remarks. His words could have been generously interpreted as "Wait right there, and I'll finish this quickly," but his callous tone angered the young Aiz. She refused to heed his command.

In a flash, she shot past him, drew her sword, and rushed straight into the horde of large, humanoid monsters known as trolls. With her slim and nimble frame, she slipped easily between their feet, slashing at their ankles and bringing them all crashing down before finishing them off with a slash from neck to breast.

Bete could hardly breathe a word before the entire horde was wiped out.

"Wha…?!"

For the first time, he beheld the Sword Princess. Not a single drop of blood marred her perfect features.

"And that's how Bete fell head over heels for our Aiz!"
"Whaaat?!"
"How?!"
"All she did was kill a few trolls!"

In the home common room, Tiona, Tione, and Lefiya were astonished by the tale that they had just heard straight from Loki's loose lips.

At a nearby table, engrossed in a card game, Aiz and Bete looked over, wondering what on earth could be causing such a commotion.

SELF-SACRIFICING SCHEMER

"*Fusillade Fallarica!!*"

"Again!"

Aiz, Tiona, and Tione watched on as spell after spell flashed before their eyes. Lefiya was training with Riveria, forced to chant again and again, barely pausing for breath.

They were on the fifth floor of the Dungeon—a necessary precaution when practicing and evaluating magic. Using magic on the surface risked damaging the city, so mages often tested their skills down here. Lefiya was no exception and had occupied a cavern in the west end of the floor for her personal use.

"Ah…!"

"Lefiya!"

After excessive spellcasting, Lefiya fell to her knees. Aiz was about to step in and help when—

"Please stay where you are, Ms. Aiz!"

"!"

"I have to push myself harder…!"

Refusing Aiz's help, Lefiya crawled to her feet and resumed her training.

According to Riveria, increasing a mage's Mind—and thereby the number of spells they could cast without rest—was much like endurance training for an athlete. No pain, no gain. However, the high elf's lessons were particularly harsh, pushing Lefiya's chanting speed to the limit. As a result, Lefiya was unsteady on her feet, and looked ready to collapse at any moment, yet she didn't yield. She kept pushing herself further and further. She wouldn't stop until she had caught up to and surpassed her friends.

"*Rea Laevateinn!!*"

As Aiz watched in suspense, Lefiya's *Summon Burst* unleashed Riveria's most powerful fire spell. Countless blazing pillars erupted, and once they sputtered out, Lefiya finally collapsed.

"Mind Down," noted Riveria. "Aiz, carry her to the Babel infirmary."

"Okay."

Aiz rushed over to Lefiya, lifting the girl's slender body onto her back.

"…She looks happy," remarked Tione, seeing the smile on the elf girl's face.

"Do you think she overdid it so that Aiz would give her a piggyback ride?" suggested Tiona.

"I do think her will to improve is real," said Riveria, "…but maybe there's more to it than that…"

Lefiya was a crafty one—always pushing herself to the limit but never forgetting to reward herself, either.

A MAIDEN NOT IN LOVE

"Captain! Wait! Come baaack!"

Tiona watched as her elder sister ran past, chasing Finn with a basket of baked sweets under her arm. After a moment, Tione seemed to notice her intense gaze and stopped in her tracks.

"...What is it?" she asked, mildly annoyed.

"Hmm...I just think it's crazy you're still going after Finn," Tiona replied.

Faced with Tione's daily antics, Tiona had to admit how much her sister had changed after meeting Finn. The old Tione would have grown bored and moved on by now.

"Hmph, that's the power of love!" boasted Tione, who fought 20, even 50 percent harder whenever Finn was watching. "Are you really saying there's not a male or two *you're* interested in?"

As Amazons could only give birth to girls, they tended to see the men of other races as potential husbands or baby-making tools, licking their lips at the sight of a strapping man even before any personal feelings factored into the matter. Rather, it was Tiona who was the odd one out, as she had so far failed to show much interest in men at all.

"I'm not saying that. It's just..." began Tiona, folding her arms. Finn wasn't her type, Bete was an automatic no, Gareth was too old for her, and Raul...well, he just wasn't boyfriend material.

...*Come to think of it, what* is *my type?*

As Tione pondered it for longer and longer, her big sister sighed and went, "Fine. I'll ask you some questions. Don't think about it too hard; just say the first thing that pops into your head. What's the first race that comes to mind?"

"Um…human!"

"Age?"

"The same as me…or younger!"

"Gender?"

"Male! …Hey, what's with that question?!"

Ignoring Tiona's objection, Tione went straight to her simplistic conclusion. "Your type is a human male no older than you!" she declared.

Tiona wasn't sure what to make of this evaluation. She pondered it for a while, her eyes turned skyward. Even with that information, she still couldn't picture her ideal man.

"Well, it doesn't matter," she concluded at last. "I don't really care about that stuff anyway."

Tiona gave a hearty laugh as her sister began to complain.

In the not-too-distant future, Tiona would finally meet an adventurer boy she could cheer for.

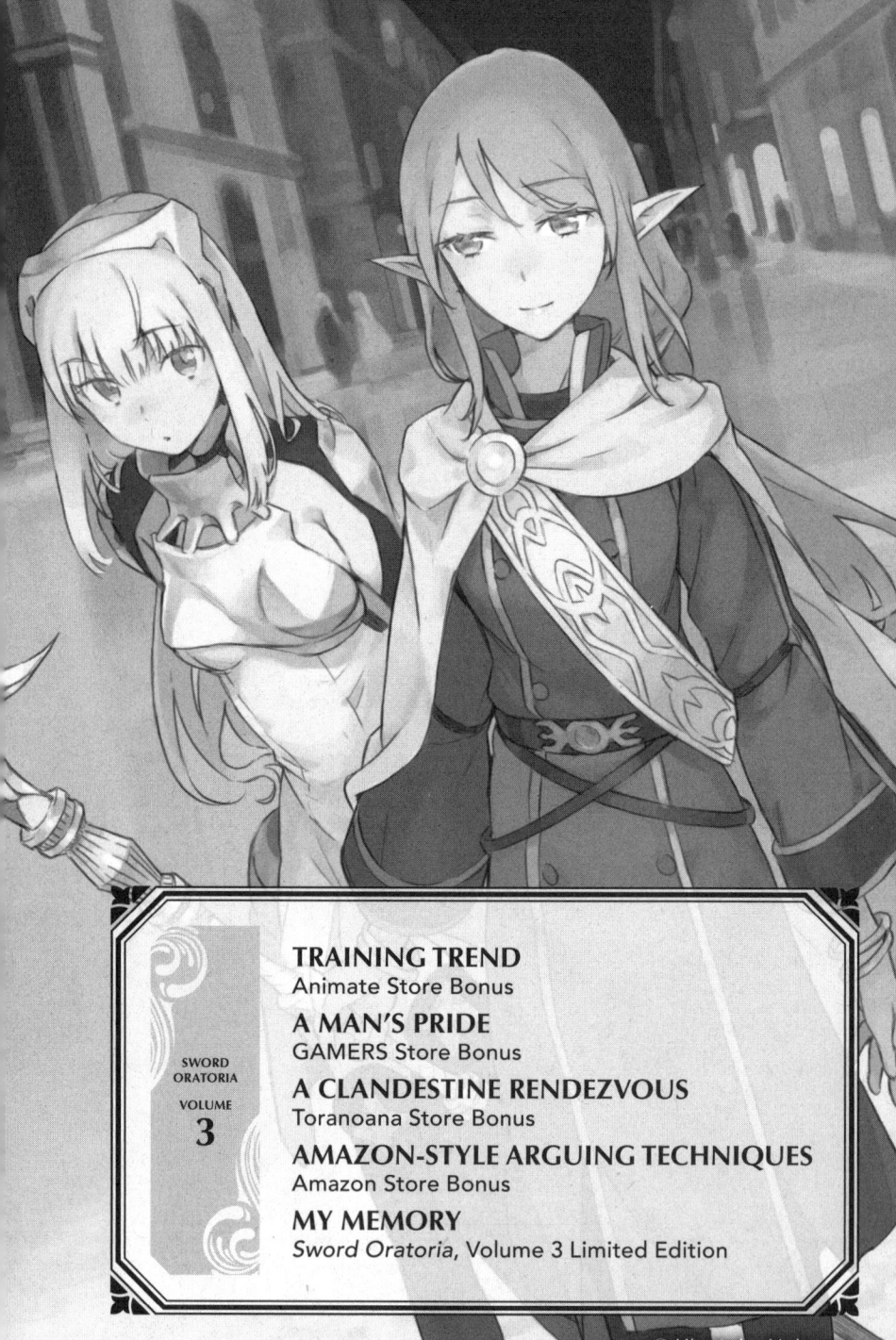

TRAINING TREND
Animate Store Bonus

A MAN'S PRIDE
GAMERS Store Bonus

A CLANDESTINE RENDEZVOUS
Toranoana Store Bonus

AMAZON-STYLE ARGUING TECHNIQUES
Amazon Store Bonus

MY MEMORY
Sword Oratoria, Volume 3 Limited Edition

SWORD ORATORIA VOLUME 3

© Kiyotaka Haimura

TRAINING TREND

"All right, let's spar!"

"You're on!"

"I'm heading to the Dungeon!"

The home of *Loki Familia* was unusually abuzz. Aiz had recently reached Level 6, inspiring the lower-ranking members to strive for similar heights, sparking a new training trend.

Even though an expedition into the deep levels was imminent, the juniors sought no rest—much to the delight and dismay of Finn and the rest of the familia leadership. Still, the top brass welcomed the increased morale, and even Loki watched over her children's progress with a grin.

"U-um...! Can I join you?"

"Sorry, Lefiya. This training is only for three people."

One by one, the other members departed until Lefiya found herself completely alone.

"Th-they all went off without me!" she groaned to herself. Suddenly, Aiz poked her head through the doorway.

"What's the matter...?" she asked.

"W-well..."

Lefiya explained her dilemma, and Aiz tilted her head.

"Why don't we train together, then?"

"Y-you really mean it?!"

Lefiya's face lit up instantly. *This is the best outcome I could have hoped for!*

A one-on-one sparring session with Aiz was more than she'd dreamed of.

"Let's play tag," Aiz suggested. "Once you tag me, we'll change places."

"Okay!"

It was a standard method meant to teach agility, evasion, and predicting your opponent's moves. Lefiya nodded happily, and the training began.

"M-Ms. Aiz...! Wait!"

Aiz zipped across the courtyard so fast she left afterimages in her wake. Lefiya gasped for breath as her legs protested. She hadn't managed to tag the Sword Princess even once. Aiz's relentless pace made Lefiya feel as if she were chasing after air.

After twelve straight hours, Lefiya finally collapsed without tagging her a single time.

A MAN'S PRIDE

An earth-shattering *thud* rattled the night.

On the outskirts of Orario, in a rented warehouse, Bete was knocked flat on his back into a pile of wooden crates. A thin line of blood ran from his lips as he stared up at the ceiling from atop the hard stones.

"Damn dwarves…You hit like a cart."

"That's not nice," replied Gareth. "I'm only doing as you asked."

Bete sat up and glared. He and another one of *Loki Familia*'s veterans were almost completely stripped down, revealing Bete's toned muscles alongside Gareth's slablike form. The former was marred with cuts and bruises, while the latter remained completely unscathed.

"Even you can't stop thinking about Aiz's success," Gareth noted. "You really are an unruly bunch, the lot of you."

When Aiz reached Level 6, it inspired the rest of the familia to train like mad. While Tiona, Tione, and Lefiya were busy bettering themselves in their own ways, Bete had called Gareth out here so they could spar alone. Yet no matter how many times he tried, Bete never managed to land so much as a scratch on the seasoned dwarf.

"Besides, I don't see the need for all this secrecy," Gareth declared. "We could train just as well on the grounds of the Twilight Manor."

"I'm not lettin' those runts back home see me gettin' my ass handed to me."

To say nothing of the embarrassment Bete clearly felt at needing to improve at all. Gareth sighed wearily at the werewolf's predictable temperament.

"Aiz…and that redheaded harpy, too. I can't let these women keep showin' me up! I'm a man, dammit!"

Bete was rude and violent, and he never spared a thought for anyone but himself. Gareth could see in the werewolf's amber eyes that nobody was more dedicated to becoming the best man he could be. He couldn't help but throw back his head and let out an eye-crinkling laugh.

"I haven't been able to let loose lately," Bete admitted. "Get ready, old man, we're going again."

"Heh. I'll put you in your place, you spoiled brat."

The old dwarf wiped the smirk from his face and readied himself for battle. He cracked his fingers and broke into a broad grin. The werewolf howl signaled the continuation of their battle. Sweat glistened in the air as fists flew beneath the watchful gaze of the full moon.

A CLANDESTINE RENDEZVOUS

In the Twilight Manor study, Finn was buried in paperwork while Riveria, his vice-captain, made conversation as she attended to her duties.

"Aiz really has lit a fire beneath the entire familia..." she said with a sigh.

"Weren't you just saying that it's good to see everyone in high spirits?" Finn replied with a wry smile.

Aiz's stunning victory against a floor boss—a feat worthy of Level 6—had left quite a strong impression. Although a Dungeon expedition was looming, everyone was busy honing themselves.

"Well, I can't say I don't know how they feel," said Finn. "I'd like to get in some practice, too, if I could." He raised a steaming mug to his lips and shot a meaningful glance at his second-in-command.

"How about it?" he asked. "When was the last time we had a spar?"

"...You'd be better off facing Gareth than a mage like me," Riveria replied curtly.

"I already asked. He's all tied up with Bete, sounds like," Finn said with a shrug. "I guess even that werewolf isn't immune to all this excitement."

Riveria sighed, closed her eyes, and smiled. "How about tonight, then? It'll be good to cut loose after all this work is done."

"Understood. I'll come to your room at midnight. Leave the door open for me."

* * *

"How about tonight, then? It'll be good to cut loose after all this work is done."

"Understood. I'll come to your room at midnight. Leave the door open for me."

As fate would have it, Lefiya and several junior members were approaching the captain's door to submit a report. When they heard the tail end of Finn and Riveria's conversation, they all blushed.

"C-Captain and Riveria...?!"

"Is that why they're always together?!"

"So the rumors were true?!"

"Keep your voice down, Leene!"

The girls immediately formed a circle and began whispering wild speculations until it was too late.

"...What did I just hear?"

"E-eep! M-Ms. Tione?!"

No one knew where she had come from, but the Amazon stood there with an unreadable look. Lefiya hurriedly tried to explain that it was probably all a big misunderstanding, but Tione was too far gone.

And so that night, a third contender managed to sneak into Finn and Riveria's clandestine rendezvous.

AMAZON-STYLE ARGUING TECHNIQUES

Lefiya was the first to notice.

""Rgh!!""

The Amazonian twins, the Hyrute sisters, were brawling in the middle of the courtyard, both covered in blood.

"M-Ms. Tiona! Ms. Tione!" she cried, running over and putting herself between them. "Please stop before you both get hurt!!"

Beaten and bloody, the two Amazonian sisters paused and turned to her with a blank stare.

"Huh? No, no, Lefiya, you've got it all wrong."

"We're sparring. We used to do it all the time back in the day."

"...What?"

Tione spat blood onto the ground as she explained.

"It's all because Aiz overtook us, you see? We're a bit frustrated right now."

"Yeah! We just wanna blow off some steam, so we thought we'd have a good, old-fashioned brawl!"

"I-I see," Lefiya replied awkwardly. "I guess I was mistaken."

They hadn't been arguing at all. The sisters, alike in more than just their looks, made perfect training partners for each other. They had been brawling since they were young—not always in good fun—and in a way, fighting their other half was like fighting themselves, constantly pushing each other to be better.

"We're the same level, and it's a much better way to gain excelia than farming monsters all the way down in the deep levels," Tiona said with a laugh. "Neither of us holds back."

Tione, who was just as battered as Tiona, added, "Besides, we go down there so often that there's nothing new about it. We have to shake things up a little, right?"

Lefiya broke into a nervous sweat at this terrifying glimpse into Amazonian culture.

"Plus," Tione continued, "everyone knows I'd win in a real fight. That's just common sense."

"What are you talking about, Sis? I'd win, obviously."

"…What?" growled Tione, narrowing her eyes while Tiona went on in a carefree tone.

"I mean, out of 999 bouts, I've won 400, and 200 have been draws."

"Did I knock something loose? There's only been 198 draws. I have more wins than you."

Tension mounted as the Amazonian sisters glared at each other. After a staredown, each raised a fist and struck the other's cheek.

""Let's settle this, right here and now!!""

"W-wait, you two!!"

The fierce fight raged on until Aiz and the others intervened.

MY MEMORY

"...Hmm?"

A tremor woke Tiona. She stared at a dark, stone ceiling, illuminated only by shafts of sunlight, streaming through the bars set in the stone walls and evenly spaced skylights overhead. The room was caked with blood and dirt, and the air was dank—far from hygienic.

Tiona lay flat on her back in the center of the room, alone. She could only smell rust and stone.

Books were strewn about, as if someone had been reading them all. Sitting up, she examined an open book that told a simple tale for children. An illustration depicted a brave hero facing a creature with a man's body and an ox's head. Perplexed, Tiona stared at it until the room shook again, and she heard voices—cheers from outside.

"Wake up. It's your turn next."

Tiona turned to see her big sister, looking much younger than she remembered.

"Tione? Why are you so small?"

"What nonsense are you spouting? Wake up, idiot. It's filthy in here."

Tione kicked a pile of books, scattering them everywhere. It was as if she had reverted to her younger self, terrible personality and all. Her usual, voluptuous figure was nowhere to be seen. Her childish body and the wild look in her sister's eyes...The raised shouts of her fellow Amazons echoing through the walls...Finally, Tiona understood.

Oh, right. This is the arena.

The Hyrute twins had been dumped here as babies, before they were even old enough to know what was going on.

Still, Tiona couldn't shake the feeling that she was missing something. She saw Tione chewing on a piece of dried meat in the corner and asked her a question.

"What did you fight today, Sis?"

"Orcs and hellhounds," Tione replied between bites, not even glancing up. "They reeked of shit and piss. I hated every second of it."

Then she jerked her chin, indicating the door she had come through. "Get moving. They said if we win today, that shitty goddess will grant us a reward."

"Really?!"

Tiona's ears perked up, and her face lit up. She sprang to her feet and sprinted from the waiting room down the hallway, undeterred by the distant roars of the arena.

What would it be today, she wondered? What triumphs awaited? What stories would be told? Thoughts of the promised reward filled her mind as she stepped through the gateless arch, into a world of light and cheering voices…

And then Tiona woke up.

"It was just a dream…"

Only the sounds of chirping birds could be heard now. Tiona sat up on her bed, looking down at the blanket she had kicked onto the floor in the night. There were no books here, only memories of the huge collection she once cherished as a child. Tiona let out a deep sigh.

"What are you going to do about your debt, Tiona?!"

That was the very first thing her big sister demanded after Tiona finished breakfast in the Twilight Manor dining hall.

"How much of that weapon do you still have to pay off?!"
"Um…About ninety million valis, I think."
"You idiot!!"
It was the day after Aiz's expedition to the twenty-fourth floor. When the Sword Princess had first reported what she encountered there, it caused quite a stir—but now all was relatively calm. Lefiya was still in bed recovering from Mind Down while Bete was up and making noise, and Aiz was nearby, so Tiona went about her normal routine while asking Aiz about her quest.

Then Tione burst in and ruined everything by getting on her case. Tiona glared at her.

"…What? What's that look for?"

"Nothing," Tiona said in a huff, opting to not comment on her sister's completely different personality compared to her dream.

"You've got to stop racking up debts!" Tione went on. "I don't care if you drag your own name through the mud, but think about how this reflects on the captain!"

"It's fine! We're all adventurers here, right, Aiz?"

"Um…"

Incidentally, Aiz was dressed in a maid outfit—Loki's punishment for going to the twenty-fourth floor without the rest of the familia. Aiz had been forced to obey her goddess's every whim while dodging her wandering hands, and now, the frilly costume drew the eyes of everyone else in the familia, making Aiz even more taciturn than usual.

"Come to think of it, Aiz, didn't you find a jewel tree on the twenty-fourth floor? Tell me where it is, and I'll go pick some treasure!"

The yield of each jewel tree varied, but finding one was a significant windfall. The green dragons that usually guarded them were no match for an adventurer of Tiona's caliber, and if she was lucky enough to get a drop item while she was at it, she could easily be looking at a profit in the region of thirty million valis.

Even a hundred-million-valis debt wasn't beyond Tiona's ability to repay. For a first-tier adventurer and member of *Loki Familia*, it was only a matter of time.

But Tiona's unrepentant attitude sent her elder sister into a rage.

"This idiot...!"

"So come on, Aiz, spill it already! Where was it?"

"Um...I think it was somewhere around—"

"Don't tell her, Aiz!"

Bang! Tione slammed her fist on the table, startling Aiz.

"This is why you keep breaking your weapons—because you think it's so easy to just buy a new one! You're a disgrace to the familia!"

"Come on, Sis! We're all adventurers here!"

"Quiet! I don't want to hear it! You're going to learn just how hard the rest of us work to make money, and we'll see if that thick head of yours can learn something, muscle brain!"

"What? And don't call me that!"

Tiona pleaded, but her sister wouldn't relent. When she said, "Well, what about the jewel tree, then? We can't just waste it," Tione simply replied, "I'll go handle it."

And so while Aiz simmered in her awkwardness, Tiona had little choice but to do the homework her big sister had given her.

"Take these goods to market and don't come back until every last thing is sold! Any money you make, you can keep."

Tione handed Tiona a bulging backpack and sent her on her way with a grin. Together with Aiz in her maid outfit, the pair saw Tiona off at the front door. Tiona departed through the manor gates, glancing back with a bitter scowl.

"Grr, why don't I get a say in this? And what's all this secondhand stuff?!"

The backpack was filled with worn-out weapons, armor, old books, and discarded clothing of every size and shape. It looked like every piece of clutter in the manor was being put up for sale because nobody could think of what else to do with them. Tiona could just imagine her sister going around asking for donations just to take credit for clearing out the trash.

"I bet she's gonna tell Finn it was her idea, too..."

Tiona thought back to the look of delight on her sister's face and sighed. Adjusting her backpack, she endured the scorching sun as she trudged toward the market in district six, nestled between West Main Street and Southwest Main Street. Here, traders flooded the city via the southwest gate, coming via Port Meren and the brackish Lolog Lake that connected Orario to the sea. With all its trading houses and marketplaces, this commercial district was the cornerstone of Orario's economy and what cemented it as the centerpiece of the modern world. Traders came by land and sea just for the chance to buy magic-stone items and other curios from the Dungeon's depths.

Tiona made her way through Central Park and turned down Southwest Main Street. The commercial district was as busy as ever. A quick glance revealed exotic fruits, fresh seafood, beautiful fabrics, and weapons forged from Damascus steel. There were more goods and people than Tiona could count.

"This'd be a lot more fun if I was buying instead of selling...!" she whined.

The district boasted the most varied sights in Orario, thanks to the many exotic traders. People wore unusual clothes that wouldn't be seen elsewhere in or around Orario, and many travelers came just to take in the sights.

Tiona found herself speculating on the background of everyone she passed in the street. *That animal person...Are they from the islands? Did that human come from the desert?* Her bulky baggage was awkward to carry, so she hoisted it above her head as she navigated the crowds. This feat of strength, akin to holding up a stocky dwarf with one hand, drew stares and murmurs from passersby.

Her destination was a specific area of the bustling commercial district. If she tried to peddle her familia's used garments at respectable establishments catering to traders and foreign dignitaries, she'd be chased out. Tiona's only option was the venue that served ordinary folks and adventurers—the flea market.

"All right, let's give this a shot!"

On her sister's advice, she picked an empty spot, laid out a cloak, and spread out the backpack's contents on it. Then she copied other vendors, calling out half-heartedly to anyone passing by.

After a few minutes, she received her first customers.

"How much is this, ma'am?" one asked.

"Um…five hundred valis, I guess?"

"That's too high! I can't afford that! How about half?"

"Mmm…Oh, fine! Take it!"

The two human women clasped their hands and celebrated finding a bargain. Tiona didn't really care what they sold for, and she steadily made more sales. Women's clothes seemed to go faster.

Oh, there goes Leene's stole…I think that brooch belonged to Rakuta…and isn't that Lefiya's dress? I guess it was getting a bit tight around her chest…She's still growing…Grr…

The clothing sold like hotcakes, and Tiona began to think that maybe this wasn't so difficult after all, but soon, the flow of customers slowed to a crawl, leaving Tiona little to do. The occasional adventurer would stop in front of her stall but most would beat a hasty retreat for some reason.

"Hey, Mord! Check out this broadsword—what a find!"

"Well, well, well. So you can still find this sorta thing at flea markets—wait, an Amazon? The Slasher?! Let's get outta here!"

"What's the big idea?" complained Tiona, pouting.

There was still unsold merchandise on the cloak and even more inside the backpack.

"Did I pick a bad spot?" she wondered aloud. "Or maybe I'm just not catching people's eyes? This gear is squeaky clean; they oughtta be selling like hotcakes, too!"

Her stall in the shade of a building near the edge of the flea market couldn't compete with the prime locations taken by more enterprising vendors. Tiona studied her rivals and quickly deduced that they went to great lengths to draw in customers or regularly changed the goods on display. She tried copying them, but it didn't make much difference.

"Oh, what's the point? I'm not cut out for this."

Exhausted, Tiona collapsed onto her back, but as self-deprecating thoughts began creeping in, her sister's grinning face appeared in her mind.

"See? I told you. Making money's not so easy. Maybe next time you'll listen to my advice."

Determined not to let Tione have the last laugh, Tiona sprang up. Perhaps a change of location was needed. She stuffed her goods into the backpack and set off.

"There's all sorts of things for sale around here," she said to herself while scouting out places to set up. There were homemade preserves, paintings, handmade trinkets—she was even shocked to see swindlers passing off random bits of claw and bone as rare Dungeon drop items. Anyone could put anything up for sale around here. The only common point was that everything was much cheaper than the regular market.

Then, just as she passed by a plaza with a water fountain, she saw it.

"Books..."

Her eyes fell on a stall run by a young elf with spectacles. Several thick books were on display. There was everything from complex philosophical treatises to medicinal field guides with lots of illustrations, all wrapped in colorful bindings. Some were laid out to reveal the covers, while others were lined up with only their spines visible.

Tiona's mind drifted back to her dream and the large collection of books she used to own as a child.

Oh, a hero story...

Her eyes were drawn to a book resting on a little easel, bearing a familiar crest. She recognized the title, written in gold letters across the leather binding: *Arcadia*.

Unable to resist, Tiona stepped over to the stall and bent down to reach for the book...when her hand brushed against another's.

""Oh!"" both of them exclaimed at the same time. Tiona turned to see who it was. However, when she did, she got an even bigger surprise, for the person was bizarrely wearing a full helm that concealed their entire face.

This mysterious individual panicked and stood back up again.

"I-I'm sorry! You take it! I don't have any money anyway..."

"Um...okay."

The voice was that of a boy, slightly too high to be fully grown. Tiona hadn't intended to purchase the book, either, but she was a bit too taken aback to manage a coherent response.

Tiona stood, noting that the boy was about her height and carried himself like an adventurer. The pitch-black helmet he wore covered everything apart from his mouth and almost made him seem like some warrior of darkness. Tiona couldn't see his eyes or the color of his hair.

After scrutinizing him for a moment, she asked the boy a question.

"Isn't it hot under there?"

Some adventurers were proud of their armor, loudly declaring it an extension of their body and wearing it wherever they went. But the only armor this boy wore was the helmet, and everything below the neck was just normal clothes. It didn't make any sense at all.

As the sun's harsh rays beat down, the boy stammered, "I...I can't take it off," he said meekly.

"...What?" replied Tiona, aghast.

In the plaza, away from the stalls, Tiona tried to piece together from the boy's account what had happened.

"So you tried it on before buying, and it got stuck?"

"Y-yeah…"

After discovering it wouldn't come off, the stall owner had forced the poor boy to pay through the teeth for the helmet, leaving him completely broke.

Without warning, Tiona grabbed the stuck helmet and pulled on it as hard as she could.

"Nnnnggrh!!"

"Owowowowowowowow!"

Despite her efforts, the helmet refused to budge, only causing the boy more pain.

If even a first-tier adventurer's strength couldn't remove it, there was only one explanation.

"It must be a cursed item!" Tiona cried, eyes wide with amazement.

"'A cursed item'?!"

Among the many magic items crafted by mages, some bore particularly unhelpful effects—cursed items. Sometimes by accident, sometimes on purpose, and lately, the result of mischievous gods ordering their followers to create them.

One common curse made it impossible to remove a piece of equipment once it was equipped. Sheer bad luck had landed this boy in his current predicament.

"I haven't seen one in a while," Tiona murmured. "…I wonder if it has any other effects."

"Um…actually," the boy replied, "it makes it so anyone I see looks…different."

"'Different'?" asked Tiona, tilting her head. "Different how?"

"Different races, different faces, that sort of thing," the boy replied. "I can't see who anyone really is. Like…for example, the man running the book stall looked like an animal person to me. What were they really?"

Tiona's eyes widened. The man at the stall had been an elf. The boy must have discovered this effect soon after donning the helmet; the stall vendor's appearance must have immediately changed from his perspective.

"Hmm...Then what do I look like?"

"Um...An elf girl," the boy replied.

"An elf? Me? Ah-ha-ha-ha-ha-ha-ha!"

Tiona burst into laughter. Elves were like the polar opposite of Amazons, and she nearly split her sides.

Now it all made sense. The reason this boy hadn't fled screaming, "Eek! Amazon the Slasher!" was because his helmet made it impossible to tell who she was.

Tiona wiped tears of laughter from her eyes while the boy stood awkwardly.

"H-how am I ever going to take this off?" he asked at last.

"Hmm...Normally, people use moly or get a mage or a healer to disenchant it..." Tiona mused aloud. She looked at the boy for a moment, then smiled. "One of my friends is a great healer! I'm sure she can break that annoying curse!"

"Y-you really mean it?!"

"However!" Tiona said, raising a finger. "First, *you* have to help *me*! I need to sell all these goods by the end of today!"

Though not exactly a lie, Tiona didn't reveal the real reason for her bargain—she didn't want to part ways with this strange boy so quickly. It was too funny that he saw her as an elf, and Tiona was secretly enjoying it. Plus, he hadn't run away screaming, which was always nice.

Most of all, the heroic tale that had brought them together stirred memories of her childhood, and she wasn't ready to let that feeling fade yet.

"How about it?" she asked, looking up at the boy. To her surprise, he immediately nodded.

"Okay," he said. "If there's anything I can do to help, then sure!"

"All right! Let's do this!"

Tiona shook his hand vigorously with both of hers, making him bob up and down.

* * *

Together, Tiona and the boy walked around the marketplace to find a good spot for their stall.

"So you like hero stories as well?" she asked.

"Yeah. My grandpa always used to read them to me. That book was one I remembered, so I reached for it without thinking..." he added bashfully. Then he realized something. "Um..."

"Hm?"

"...What's your name? I just realized I haven't asked."

Tiona hesitated—she usually didn't mind giving her name, but for whatever reason, she wanted to keep the masquerade going a bit longer.

"Elna," she said. "My name's Elna."

"Isn't that...the same as in that book?"

"Ah-ha-ha! Figures you'd know!"

Elna was the name of a character in the novel *Arcadia*—the very book they had just seen. Though the boy likely suspected it was a lie, he still went along with it.

"So Ms. Elna, how did you get into hero tales?" he asked.

"I didn't realize it at the time, but I had a pretty troubled childhood," Tiona replied. "I didn't enjoy much besides fighting. But one day, I picked up an old book someone left lying around—and I was hooked..."

That old book had been little more than a bundle of scrap paper. Back then, when the young girl's life consisted of nothing but fighting monsters and other Amazons, the story contained in those pages offered a thrill she had never known. She could still remember that feeling like it was yesterday.

Realizing her words had stunned the boy into silence, Tiona hastily changed the subject.

"So anyway, you said I look like an elf, right? What kind?"

"U-um...right. Well, you've got, er...blond hair."

"Yeah?"

"Long."

"Ooh!"

"Your eyes are..."

This went on for a while. It turned out that even Tiona's voice and clothing appeared differently to the boy. As far as he could tell, she was as modestly dressed as any elf in a dress and a cape and spoke in a soothing soprano.

Tiona couldn't help but giggle. *That sounds just like Lefiya! What a hoot!*

After a short search, they found a decent spot and set up shop. While doing so, Tiona pressed the boy for more details. He explained that his supporter had recently gone missing. After checking everywhere without success, a friend brought him here, to the flea market, to take his mind off the matter. After his mishap with the helmet, he'd somehow gotten separated from this friend, which was how he ended up meeting Tiona.

When Tiona asked if he wasn't worried about his missing supporter, he admitted he was, but he had a feeling she would show up again, like she always did.

Tiona sensed the bond of trust between them, and a smile spread across her face.

They finished setting up Tiona's goods and continued chatting as they waited for customers.

After about an hour of no sales, Tiona yelled, "...Nobody's buying anything at all!"

They'd tried calling out to customers, but anyone who recognized Tiona ran away. She was starting to think the issue wasn't the quality of her wares but her reputation. She sighed as she looked at her stall standing in the shade of a building.

"Um..." said the boy. "Do you think maybe we should take the initiative and go find buyers?"

"How do you mean?"

"Well, it's like trading magic stones. We could pay other stalls a visit."

It wasn't uncommon for vendors to buy merchandise from other stalls and resell it for a profit. While this sometimes annoyed the original sellers, it was seen as mostly their own fault for underestimating the value of their wares. By buying low and selling high, an enterprising individual could achieve an income comparable to an adventurer. They were the kinds of people who referred to the flea market as a treasure trove of bargains.

"Does that mean we'll have to haggle?" Tiona asked. "I'm not really confident about that, but…Hmm…"

Bargaining was a standard tool for adventurers negotiating prices when they sold their Dungeon loot to merchants and commerce-focused familias. Given the number of stalls in the flea market, it wouldn't be that hard to find some success. While Tiona couldn't match Raul and her other peers in this field, she also couldn't deny wanting to see the look on her sister's face if she went home with a mountain of valis.

After a moment of thought, she decided, "Let's give it a try! It can't be any worse than sitting around here selling nothing!"

The best defense is a good offense—Tiona had lived by that motto her whole life. Stuffing her goods back into her bag, she set off with the boy to improve her flea-market career. Scanning the stalls, she picked one with a solid wooden structure that looked a bit more upscale and marched right up to it.

After presenting her goods to the Amazon behind the counter…

"Nothing too special. I'll give you a thousand valis for the lot."

"Whaaat?! That's way too little!"

For twenty-odd articles of clothing, that was a miserable sum. Tiona figured she could practically give them away and earn more than that.

"Come on! Help a sister out! You can go higher than that, can't you?"

"Sorry, but I've got bills to pay, just like everyone else!"

"But look at these battle clothes! They're basically new!"

"I'm still not paying more than that for some old books and hand-me-downs!"

The stall owner's name turned out to be Lulu, and she refused to budge on the price. She knew exactly how much power she held in this negotiation.

Lulu possessed rather babyish looks for an Amazon, with a sugary voice and voluptuous physique. Although she was about her sister's height, Lulu was considerably better endowed, and to compare her assets to Tiona's was simply cruel.

Tiona felt defeated in more ways than one. She simply didn't have anything to bargain with, and her face was turning red with embarrassment.

Just then, the boy timidly suggested, "Um…what about if I add in this equipment?"

"Well, well…" Lulu had a very different look in her eyes now.

Tiona went, "Oh yeah, I forgot that," when she saw what the boy had placed on the counter—a dully gleaming broadsword and a chipped shield. The owner had outgrown them. Still, they were perfectly serviceable, even if they probably wouldn't survive one of *Loki Familia*'s expeditions. Lulu's reaction made it clear they were still valuable.

"Could you raise the price a little if we threw these in…?"

Tiona later heard that the boy had recently bought a pair of potions: a cheap one and an expensive magic one. That experience had taught him that bundling unwanted items with a premium one could fetch a better price, and this was his first attempt at trying out that strategy for himself.

Tiona didn't miss Lulu flinching when the boy made his suggestion. The equipment he had offered might even garner the interest of a deep-pocketed, high-street vendor, and Lulu seemed willing to go to great lengths to obtain them.

"H-hmm…Well, I suppose I could part with maybe thirty thousand…"

"Three hundred thousand!!" Tiona countered, recalling the time her sister sold the Cadmus Hide. Lulu's eyes widened in shock, and even the boy's helmet couldn't hide his surprise.

"You must be joking! I'll never pay that much!!"

"Then I guess I'll take my business someplace else!"

Lulu gnashed her teeth in frustration, and Tiona was delighted—the shoe was on the other foot now. The two Amazons glared at each other while the boy struggled to recover from his shock.

"...Fine," Lulu said. "I'll pay." She finally relented and dropped a bag of coins onto the counter. However, she was wearing a defiant grin. Tiona was momentarily confused, but then Lulu rose to her feet and declared, "On one condition! You'll have to buy some of my goods, and the cost will come out of what I pay you!"

"...What? Why would we do that?"

Tiona wasn't a fan of this idea, but Lulu's smug grin said it all. She walked around to the front of the stall, and as she passed the helmeted boy, she took his hand and squeezed it. While Tiona and the boy exchanged confused shrieks, Lulu bent down, blushed, and in an even sweeter voice than before, asked, "Hey, little boy, won't you give me a discount?"

With her eyes upturned, her body pressed against his, her cleavage right in the boy's face, Lulu did everything she could to sway him.

"If you do what I want...then I'll let you have some fun with me."

What a horrible woman!!

Tiona was on the verge of violent eruption. This damn cougar was using her charms to get her way! It wasn't fair!

Lulu was well aware that her body was her most effective weapon, and she was using it on the boy to great effect. She would get him to make a promise, let him brush a tit or something, and drive down the asking price!

It was scandalous! Disgraceful! And a blatant attack on Tiona's assets!!

She'd just started to open her heart to the boy, and now he was being stolen right from under her nose. She felt so angry and defeated that she couldn't stop the boy before he timidly opened his lips.

"...I'm...good," he answered hoarsely. "I-I think I'll pass..."

"...Huh?"

Lulu froze, clearly unprepared for a refusal. Tiona was momentarily speechless, too, but when she saw the boy slip out of Lulu's grip and take a few steps back, she grinned triumphantly.

"Ha-hah! Your dirty tricks won't work on us! Now hand over that money!!"

"Wh-why? Why aren't you interested? Are you saying...I'm not good enough?!"

Lulu collapsed to her knees and began to sob, while Tiona snatched the sack of coins off the counter and stuck out her tongue. Then she grabbed the boy's hand and ran off.

"Ah-ha-ha-ha-ha-ha! It feels good to come out on top!!"

"Ha...ha-ha-ha..."

After running a good distance, Tiona stopped, turned, and beamed at the boy.

"But I'm impressed," she said. "How did you turn that Amazon down? Even I could tell she was super sexy."

Tiona's question seemed to throw the boy for a loop. After a long pause, he replied. "...She was an Amazon?"

"Oh, right," Tiona said, remembering the cursed helmet prevented him from seeing people as they really were. "What did she look like, then? Don't tell me she was a man!"

"Erm...no, she was a woman..." the boy replied, unsure how to proceed. He walked over to Tiona and whispered the remainder in her ear. "A really burly dwarf woman..."

At that stunning revelation, Tiona burst out laughing.

Once Tiona's task was finished, it was time for her to hold up her end of the bargain. She roamed the flea market in search of a healer who could remove the helmet's curse.

"Hm? Isn't that…? Hey! Amid!!"

Tiona's keen eyes picked out a head of silver hair among the crowd. She ran over, waving.

"Ms. Tiona?" Amid called, turning around.

"I didn't know you were here at the flea market, too!"

When Tiona had mentioned she knew a great healer who could tackle curses, this was the person she had in mind.

"My patron god let me take a break, so I came here to relax…" Amid explained.

"Perfect!" replied Tiona, and she quickly explained the situation. By the time the boy caught up, Amid's gaze turned to him. "I see," she muttered. "In that case, please come to my store. I should be able to—"

"What are you doing to my customer, Amid?" a resentful voice interrupted.

Tiona spun around to see a chienthrope holding a large paper bag.

"…Nahza Ersuisu," Amid said, recognizing the girl.

"Haven't you stolen enough from us already?" Nahza asked flatly, peering out from behind the overflowing bag of medicinal ingredients in her arms. "This customer is mine."

"M-Ms. Nahza?" the boy stammered. "How did you know it was me? And, huh, you've become an elf, too."

"Yeah, I recognized your smell," Nahza replied. "I don't know what you mean about becoming an elf, though."

Tiona realized that the mysterious person who had brought the boy to the flea market and then disappeared must have been Nahza. The chienthrope girl approached him and gave him a sniff. After Tiona explained the situation once more, Nahza took the boy by the hand and began to lead him away.

"Let's go," she said. "We don't need to bother Dian Cecht with this. I'll take care of this curse with my potions...It'll cost you, though."

"W-wait! Ms. Nahza!"

"...!"

Tiona's arm shot out...then dropped weakly as she watched the boy turn and bob his head apologetically before being dragged away into the crowd, leaving her alone with Amid.

"Do you know that chienthrope girl?" Tiona asked.

"Yes, our paths have crossed a few times," Amid replied. "I don't think she likes me very much."

It was strange to see the silver-haired healer so ambivalent about someone. She sighed, and Tiona sensed she didn't want to talk about it.

Tiona was sad to see the boy go, but she understood that all good things had to come to an end. Then she realized something.

"Oh."

"What's wrong, Ms. Tiona?"

"I forgot to ask for his name..."

Spending an enjoyable afternoon together without ever knowing each other's names—it was just like something out of a romance novel, and Tiona couldn't help but chuckle. She felt like she'd gained another precious item for her collection.

Perhaps their paths would cross again someday. With that in mind, Tiona retraced her steps. "Amid, will you come do some shopping with me?"

"Very well, but what are you buying?" Amid replied. Tiona blushed and donned a broad smile as memories of her childhood came flooding back.

"An old book that turned into a memory," she answered.

EVEN SAINTS DON'T KNOW EVERYTHING
Animate Store Bonus

WHO IS YOUR RIVAL?
GAMERS Store Bonus

SUPER SMASH ADVENTURERS
Toranoana Store Bonus

ATTACK AND DEFENSE ON THE EVE OF WAR
Amazon Store Bonus

SWORD ORATORIA VOLUME 4

© Kiyotaka Haimura

EVEN SAINTS DON'T KNOW EVERYTHING

"Um, Amid…do you have a minute?"

The healer of *Dian Cecht Familia* tilted her head at Aiz's question. It was past dusk, and she was in the middle of closing up shop. *What could bring her here at this hour?* she wondered, leading Aiz inside so that the two of them could speak privately.

Just as Amid recalled that *Loki Familia* was meant to go on an expedition soon, Aiz spoke up and divulged the reason for her visit.

"Could you teach me…how to do first aid?"

"'First aid'? I'm not trying to pressure you to buy anything, but what's wrong with using potions?"

"Um, I don't really want to use too many potions just for training…" Aiz muttered, and Amid, understanding where the girl was coming from, beamed a gentle smile.

Amid was already nineteen, though at not even 150 celches high, she seemed much younger. She'd made a name for herself as a healer and was no stranger to the Dungeon, being Level 2. As part of a mission to clear a floor boss, she once single-handedly bolstered a faltering front line with her unique magic, earning her the alias Dea Saint.

Amid couldn't hide the pride she felt at the fact that a younger adventurer was coming to her for help and advice.

"Um, Amid. There's one other thing…"

"Go ahead. Whatever it is, if I can help, I shall."

Seeing her saintly smile, Aiz steeled herself and asked.

"What's the right way to give someone a lap pillow?"

"Erm, what?"

The sudden non sequitur threw Amid for a loop. She had given a lap pillow before, but only to a unicorn, and she wasn't sure there was any right or wrong way to do it.

The more she looked at Aiz's reddening face, the more her own cheeks started to blush. She wanted to throw up her hands in defeat, but when she looked into those expectant, trusting eyes, there was nothing else she could do.

She looked from side to side, sweating, then finally nodded.

"V-very well," she said. "I shall teach you the basics. Please set your head in my lap, if you don't mind…"

"Lord Dian Cecht, I just visited Amid's room, and it seems she is giving a lap pillow to the Sword Princess."

"Why are you telling me this? And why is your nose bleeding?"

The god's follower replied with a blithe look. "See for yourself. It's quite the sight…" he said.

A few days later, the rumors had gotten quite out of hand, and more than a few gods showed up, knocking and demanding, "Where's the yuri?!" Unfortunately, nobody knew quite what they were talking about.

WHO IS YOUR RIVAL?

"Lady Riveria? May I ask a question about this chant here?"

"Ah…Sure…"

Riveria looked at Lefiya and the magical textbook in her hand before giving a gentle nod. It was late at night in the Twilight Manor, and Riveria's study was filled with plans for the upcoming expedition.

Lefiya had been coming to her regularly with questions for some days now, and though it was completely dark outside, the light of the magic-stone torches was more than enough to see the lifeless look in Lefiya's eyes. It seemed like every day she spent the daylight hours training, only to return in the evening to seek Riveria's advice. Her willingness to learn was impressive…and more than a little concerning.

"Lefiya…are you sleeping properly?"

"Of course. I make sure to get one hour every night."

"You fool, we have an expedition coming up!" Riveria roared. The Falna enhanced an adventurer's mental and physical capabilities, but there were limits. It was important to not overdo it, especially before a big mission, but Lefiya didn't seem to be listening. She was staring silently at the words on the page instead.

Well, at least she's making an effort.

Lefiya had always been eager to catch up to Aiz, but recently, she seemed possessed by something new—something that had driven her to be far more diligent, and even reckless, in her studies than ever before. Perhaps she had gained a rivalry with someone, Riveria thought, smiling.

After some instruction, Lefiya seemed to understand, and she thanked Riveria, bowed, and turned to leave the room. As she reached the doorframe, however, she stopped.

"Lady Riveria?" she asked. "Pardon the sudden question, but…is it true that people in the past used to sacrifice rabbits to put curses on people?"

"Yes, that's right. Witches used rabbits as ingredients in potions and magic items. Why do you ask?"

Lefiya stared at the floor for a moment, then raised her head.

"Then what do you do if you want to curse a rabbit?"

"What kind of creature are you fighting against…?"

The look in her student's eyes seemed wearier than ever. Riveria sighed. Sometimes she just didn't understand this girl.

SUPER SMASH ADVENTURERS

Twentieth floor.
"RAAAAAAAAAAAAAAAGHHH!!"
Twenty-fifth floor.
"GRAAAAAAAAAAAAAGHHH!!"
Thirtieth floor.
"AAAAAAAAAAAAAAAAAAAAAAARGHH!!"
"WRAAAAAAAAAAAAAAAAAAAAAAGHHH!!"
Fortieth floor.
"""OUT OF MY WAAAAAAAAAAAAAAAAAAAAAAA AYYY!!"""

The bodies of fallen Irregulars littered the Dungeon floor. Bete and Tiona pushed on, Frosvirt and Urga swinging, screaming at anyone and anything that came between them and their prey.

It was the fourth day of the expedition. Their encounter with a certain adventurer boy on the upper levels had driven these two completely mad, causing them to attack every monster they could find. The junior members of the party were left with nothing to do but watch in awe. It was as if Bete and Tiona had forgotten there was an expedition going on at all.

"E-erm…excuse me, you two?"

"What?!"

"What is it?!"

"E-erm, it's just that…Tione's over there fighting monsters by herself…"

""What?!""

Following Raul's trembling finger, the crazed adventurers spotted Tiona's sister, consumed by the same bloodlust. Eager not to let the Amazon steal their kills, the two dashed off to join her.

Back at the commander's formation, the leaders of *Loki Familia* watched—their subordinates, on the warpath, and Aiz, standing on the sidelines, itching to be a part of it.

"...If Aiz joins them, I don't know what we'll do," said Gareth with a sigh.

"At least they're dealing with all the monsters by themselves," added Riveria.

"...I think I'm getting a migraine," said Finn.

Elsewhere, Raul was approached by Tsubaki, leading her contingent of *Hephaistos Familia* members.

"Ha-ha-ha!" she chuckled. "You sure are a lively bunch!"

"Tell me about it..." moaned Raul.

ATTACK AND DEFENSE ON THE EVE OF WAR

"M-Ms. Tione, are you sure about this?"

"We won't be long! I just want to see his sleeping face, and then we'll be gone!"

You're definitely planning to get in bed with him!

On the Dungeon's fiftieth floor, Tione made her way through the *Loki Familia* camp, stealthily avoiding the watchful eyes of the lookouts, with Lefiya reluctantly in tow. Tione's destination: the large tent where her prum captain was sleeping.

The following morning, *Loki Familia* would commence their expedition into uncharted territory, and Tione was so excited she couldn't sleep. To subdue her primal instincts, she wanted to spend the night with her beloved captain, and Lefiya, who had been sleeping in the same tent as her, had been dragged along for the ride.

And so, giggling maniacally at the thought of using her bantam leader as a body pillow, Tione carefully made her way to the captain's tent.

"I-I really don't think we should do this!" Lefiya said. "Let's go back!" But her warnings went unheeded as Tione marched through the front flap.

"And what might you be here for?"

"R-Riveria?!"

"Lady Riveria!"

Inside the tent, Tione found not the sleeping face of her beloved captain but instead the ice-cold glare of his high-elf aide.

"Wh-what's going on? Where's the captain?!"

"Finn said his thumb was aching, so he went to sleep in a different tent. I never imagined you two would be the cause. We have an important job on the morrow, you know!"

"Wahh! I wasn't going to do anything—I swear!" wept Lefiya, but before she could get another word out, Riveria dropped the hammer. A cry of "Captaaaaaain!!" echoed across the camp, and the two little intruders fled back to their tent, where they went straight to sleep without another peep.

"Are you really going to sleep in our tent, Finn?"

"I'm afraid so. Sorry to be a bother."

At the other end of the camp, Finn was sharing his lodgings with the blacksmiths of *Hephaistos Familia*. There was an indescribable look in his eye as he made his apologies to Tsubaki.

"Heh-heh-heh. In that case," Tsubaki replied, "you'll have to be my body pillow for the night."

"Oh, bugger."

Braver had just made the greatest mistake of his life.

LET ME JOIN IN
Animate Store Bonus

A DOG'S PAYBACK?
GAMERS Store Bonus

INTRUDERS WILL BE MERCILESSLY CURSED
Toranoana Store Bonus

ROYALTY AND RESPECT
Generic Store Bonus

SWORD ORATORIA VOLUME 5

© Kiyotaka Haimura

LET ME JOIN IN

"Hey, Argonaut! Remember what we were talking about yesterday?"

"Oh, Tiona. Yes, of course, what is it?"

Tiona and Bell began chatting—while Aiz watched them like a hawk. It was just after breakfast, the morning after the rescue team returned to the eighteenth floor, and Bell had nothing to do. It was then that Tiona came bounding up to him, a huge smile on her face, bumping shoulders and getting chummy, much to Aiz's chagrin.

For some reason, the closeness bothered her. It was as if a beloved pet had started cuddling with someone else instead. Aiz didn't know if that made her feel lonely or sad, but at any rate, she didn't like it.

After a while, she worked up her courage and marched right up to the overly intimate pair. She had to get in between them somehow…

"Do you know the one where Elna of Arcadia meets the masked knight? And she never finds out his name until she leaves?"

"Um…I'm not sure I know that one. But if we're talking about *Arcadia*, then I know the story of the Skeleton King…"

I…don't know any of them!

A shiver shot down Aiz's spine. Her mother had told her many tales as a child, so Aiz figured she was well-equipped to tackle the discussion, but she had been mistaken. Sweat dribbled down her brow as she recalled Loki's words: *"There's some real die-hard freaks called* otaku *in this world!"*

She hung around, eavesdropping, waiting for a chance to enter the conversation, when…

"How about the story of the Sleeping Princess? I really like how—"

A chance! Recognizing a familiar title, Aiz stepped in.

"I know that one!" she yelled.

Tiona and Bell turned to look at her, wearing faces of utter bewilderment. Slowly, it dawned on Aiz what an embarrassing thing she'd just done, and *poof*! Her face turned an uncharacteristic shade of scarlet.

"Um…I…er…that is to say…I…"

Aiz stared at the ground, mumbling nonsense in a voice so quiet it might have gone out like a candle flame.

So cute.

So cute.

Tiona turned to her and smiled, while Bell covered his mouth with his hands, his whole face flushing.

A DOG'S PAYBACK?

"Tch. Still not enough, huh?"

"This stuff ain't easy to find..."

Bete and Loki roamed the sunlit streets of Orario, trying to gather enough antivenin for their colleagues on the eighteenth floor, but it was harder than expected. The poison vermis was only found on the lower levels, and even then, it was not particularly common. Outside of Irregular occurrences, like the mass spawn *Loki Familia* ran into, the creatures were rather rare, and by extension, so were their drop items.

"We've checked every store that might have 'em," growled Bete. "All that's left is to hope the other familias have some stock they're willin' to trade..."

"As if it's gonna be that easy." Loki sighed. "They'll take one look at the mess we're in and make us pay through the nose—if they let us have 'em at all."

There was no shortage of rivals and resentful adventurers who had it in for one of the city's most powerful familias. Word would have spread that Loki's children were looking for antivenin, and anyone with inventory was probably drooling at the thought of the high prices they could charge. Of course, money was no object when it came to her familia's safety, but negotiations were going to take a great deal of time, which was something currently in very short supply.

Bete clicked his tongue a second time as he thought about what troubles awaited.

"If only there was someone who would cut us a deal and put in a good word to the other familias and merchants as well..." Loki mused.

The ears on the top of Bete's head twitched.

"Loki," he said. "Go back to the manor. Call everybody and get the shit together."

"Oh? You think of somethin'?"

"Just go," barked Bete as he headed off by himself to another part of the city.

"Erk. Vanargand?"

Lulune winced when she saw who had just barged into the *Hermes Familia* home. Bete explained the situation and ordered her to gather up every vial of antivenin she had.

"Don't forget how we saved all your asses on the twenty-fourth floor," he said.

"I-I know, but still...!" the chienthrope girl whined. "Neither Lord Hermes nor Asfi are here right now, so we can't just give them to you!"

As the argument played out in the entrance hall, a prum girl and weretiger man watched on from a safe distance.

"Keep talkin', and I'll tell the Guild about how you fudge your levels," Bete growled.

"Th-that's not fair!"

In the end, Lulune had no choice but to comply with Bete's demands, landing her in hot water when Hermes and Asfi eventually returned.

INTRUDERS WILL BE MERCILESSLY CURSED

"Ms. Tione? Do you know any reliable methods to purge unwanted intruders?"

"What in the world made you ask such a scary question?"

Loki Familia had made their camp on the eighteenth floor. It was the night of Bell and Hestia's arrival, and Tione had just wrapped up a meeting after Hermes appeared. She was on her way back to her tent when Lefiya approached her, dripping with hostility.

"Well," began the elf, "the truth is, an undesirable has begun hanging around someone very dear to me. I was wondering if there might be a way to eradicate them entirely."

"What's this, jealousy? Really, Lefiya, you should really put silly things like—"

"How would you feel if there was somebody you didn't like hanging around the captain?"

"Murderous rage." All of a sudden, there was no light in Tione's eyes anymore. "If any rutting whores tried to seduce my captain, I'd rip them limb from limb," she said. "I wouldn't allow a single one of them to contaminate my beloved."

"But our loved ones are kind, generous people. They wouldn't want to see things become violent. What should we do?"

"Hrmm. How annoying. How dare they take advantage of the captain's kindness like that..."

Lefiya and Tione went on and on, raving over the imagined enemies they had each conjured in their minds.

"Perhaps we could take them by surprise, ambush them...No, if the captain gets even a whiff of foul play, he'll trace it back to me. I could threaten them to stay away, but there's no guarantee they'll stay silent..."

"If words won't work, then perhaps we can use a different way to convince them to stay away. Curse them so bad that something terrible happens if they come near..."

"That's it! We can curse them! That way, it can't be traced back to us!!"

"Now that I think about it, Lady Riveria told me that rabbits were once used to cast curses...!"

"Lefiya, if you find out how to do it, can you teach me, too?! Then all those harlots after the captain will...Hee-hee-hee-hee-hee!"

"Please, Gareth. Can't you do something about her?"

"It's not my business. You're the captain; you should step in."

Watching the elf and the Amazon slowly descend into madness, Finn pleaded with his dwarven aide and closest friend. Clutching his stomach, he looked on with despair. It seemed his troubles were far from over.

ROYALTY AND RESPECT

"If you'll excuse me, I shall go perform my ablutions."

It was the night of Bell's arrival on the eighteenth floor. After parting with Finn, Riveria took her leave and left the camp under cover of darkness. She was on her way to the forest spring to bathe, and the last thing she wanted was for the other members of her race to spot her. If they did, there would be no end of eager elves lining up to wait on her hand and foot. Riveria had experienced enough royal treatment to last a lifetime.

However, her optimism was short-lived. She only made it a few steps out of camp before she heard…

"Please allow me to accompany you, Lady Riveria!"

"Me too!"

"I-I'll come as well!"

When Riveria turned around, she was greeted by a long procession of elves headed by the Level 4 adventurer Alicia, including a gaggle of female mages. Even Lefiya was there. Riveria rubbed the bridge of her nose and sighed.

"How many times must I tell you?" she groaned. "I do not wish to be treated like royalty."

"But Lady Riveria, even so. The forest at night is filled with dangerous men…I mean, monsters. We simply cannot let you go by yourself!"

""""""Let us come with you!"""""""

Riveria sighed and, sensing any further argument would be a

waste of effort, allowed the elves to accompany her. They all bowed deeply and followed her closely. Not long after, the group arrived at their destination—a hidden spring nestled among mountain crags, like some undiscovered natural wonder.

The elves immediately took up a defensive formation around their liege, and Riveria sighed as she began to disrobe. She undid her hairpin, allowing a beautiful stream of jade-green hair to flow down her back. Lefiya and the other elves gasped in wonder as she slipped into the pool.

Then, as she began to wash herself, an unknown figure stepped into view.

"Wh-who's there?!" the lookouts cried, and at their voices, the shadow slipped away back into the forest. While the elves worked themselves into a frenzy over the appearance of this intruder, Riveria's mind remained fixed on the trespasser's face, which only she had seen.

That was…the masked adventurer from the rescue team. I'm sure of it.

Upon investigation, there was a small jug of water and a rolled-up parchment left on the forest floor where the figure had been spotted.

"It's…Alv Spring Water! I'd…er…I'd better make sure it's not poisoned!"

"Alicia! That's not fair!"

"She's going to drink it all!"

"Of course not! I'm only doing this for Lady Riveria!"

The elves immediately started quarreling over the beverage, a dear luxury this far from the surface. Meanwhile, Riveria stepped out of the pool and examined the scroll. In prim and tidy letters, it read, *To a noble and respected high elf*. Riveria looked at it and the accompanying tribute and began to wonder.

"The masked adventurer…Just who are you, really?"

LATER ON, AT A SMALL RESTAURANT

"Come on, Lefiya, you promised you'd take me out someplace nice to eat!"

Two days after settling their business with the island nation of Telskyura, but before returning to Orario, Aiz, Lefiya, and the Hyrute sisters stayed in the port town of Meren at Tiona's request.

"Scotta?" asked Tiona, reading the sign out front. "Is this the place?"

"Yes!" replied Lefiya with enthusiasm. "Their beef stew is amazing! Their prices are a little steep, but many famous writers are said to have dined here!"

It was clearly a place with a history, and the smells wafting from inside signaled the restaurant's virtues better than any review could. When the group entered, however, they came face-to-face with two people they didn't expect.

"Kali?! Bache?!" cried Tione upon seeing the childlike goddess and her sandy-haired captain. "What are you doing here?!"

Kali seemed just as surprised to see the Hyrutes as they were to see her. "We aren't looking for a fight," she replied, noting the swiftness with which Tione readied herself for battle. "We lost. It's over. I'm just here to enjoy a nice meal with Bache."

After a moment, Tione relaxed her guard. Meanwhile, Tiona glanced around and tilted her head.

"Hm? Where's Argana?" she asked. Kali and Bache both stared off into the distance, saying nothing.

Keeping a safe distance, the group sat down at the next table over and placed their orders.

"Well, whatever," said Tiona. "You're right: It's all over now, so no hard feelings, yeah? I'm still riding the high from beating Bache!"

Tiona hadn't meant anything by it, and Bache remained silent, but her eye twitched in indignation, nonetheless. After a while, four steaming bowls of stew were placed on the table, eliciting *oohs* and *aahs* from the girls of *Loki Familia*.

Then...

"*Algu!*"

An instant later, every bowl was completely empty. The stew had disappeared down Bache's gullet. The eyes of *Loki Familia* were reduced to dots.

Bache lifted her mouth covering and licked her lips. She then raised two fingers and beckoned the twins, taunting them. This may not have been a fight, but it was a battle—and Bache hated losing.

The Hyrute twins growled, their desire for war reignited.

"Get me one more beef stew!!"

"Stewed tongue for me!! Five orders!!"

"Tiona?! Tione?! Settle down! This isn't that kind of place!!"

Amid the chaos, Kali approached Aiz with an offer.

"Hey, Sword Princess, how about you come back to Telskyura with us? You can fight all you want."

"I'm not sure how I feel about killing other people to get stronger..."

"Hold on! Are you trying to steal Ms. Aiz away?! I won't allow it!!"

Three Amazons were gearing up for battle, the Sword Princess was getting recruited by another goddess, and one elf was on the verge of losing her patience when the store owner stepped in.

"All of you, get the hell out of my shop!!" he roared.

IT'S TOUGH BEING POPULAR

In the Twilight Manor's study, Finn was sitting in his chair. Through his window, he could see the sun set in the west and give way to dusk. Finn sighed, stopped scribbling with his quill pen, and looked around the empty room.

"I don't think this room has ever seemed so large…"

Loki and many of her children had left for Port Meren three days prior. There was no Riveria to grant him assistance and no Tiona to break into his room and follow him around everywhere. Thanks to that, he had made more progress on his work than ever before, but Finn found little satisfaction in the stack of completed paperwork that had piled up on his desk.

"Excuse me, Finn," said Gareth, entering the study. "Sorry to be a bother, but could you look over this contract with *Hephaistos Fami*—Hm? Why the long face? Missing the rascals already, are you?"

"Is it that obvious?" Finn smiled. "If I am, old friend, then there must be something seriously wrong with me. You know, when you entered just now, for a moment, I thought it might be one of them."

"Hmph! Then your symptoms must be getting worse!" joked Gareth.

Just then, there was a cry of "Captain!!" and someone came running into the study—someone whom Finn was sure he had seen off just three days prior.

"Aki, what's the matter?" he asked. "Did something happen?"

"A message from Loki! It's Tione and Tiona! They…"

The catgirl breathlessly explained the situation, and Finn's eyes, as clear and blue as the surface of a lake, narrowed in an instant.

"Gareth," he said, standing up from his seat. "Gather all our people. Go into town and collect everybody's gear, no matter what state of repair they're in. We're going to Meren."

"Understood, but Bete and a few of the others went to the bar. They could be anywhere in the city."

"Then go to the walls and fly our emergency banner. Let every mortal and deity in the city know that all members of *Loki Familia* are to convene at the walls immediately."

Finn's swift decisions spurred the whole familia into action. The prum commander picked up his weapon, the Fortia Spear, and exited into the hallway.

"Heh. I should have known better than to expect a quiet moment," he said. "Even when you're not around, you're still giving me grief."

The momentary smile on Finn's lips was quickly replaced with the stern, determined frown of a captain, and he set off to extricate his juniors from their latest troubles.

TRAUMATIC MEMORIES OF DAYS GONE BY

"Wait right there, Aiz! What about your swimming lessons?"
Not this again...
Those were the young Aiz's thoughts when Riveria began upbraiding her.
"Finn said I could practice fighting with him..."
"Did you forget you're with me today? We can't have you sinking like a stone forever, you know!"
It was about nine years before the present day, and Riveria had just stopped the seven-year-old Aiz from tiptoeing out of the manor, shortsword in hand.
"But swimming won't help me in a battle..." Aiz pouted.
"Oh, it will. Let's drop you in a pool of kelpies and see what happens, shall we?"
Aiz hadn't always gotten on so swimmingly with the other members of *Loki Familia*—Riveria least of all. She was a rebellious child, only concerned with improving her skill with the blade, and perhaps that was why Riveria took it upon herself to act like the girl's mother. Not a day went by when the high elf couldn't be heard scolding the young girl over one fault or another.
"It's all well and good to focus on your strengths," she went on, "but it's equally important to work on eliminating your weaknesses. Having a well-rounded education will serve you well in—"
And so on. Nag, nag, nag, nag, nag, until even the unexpressive

Aiz was beginning to show signs of annoyance. Riveria's sermon went on and on, with no end in sight, until…

"Okay, *Grandma*…"

The elf's long ears twitched, and Riveria glowered at Aiz with a look as cold as ice.

"It looks like you need to learn just how frightening the waters can be, young lady," she said, "…and hopefully pick up some manners in the process."

"…And poor Aiz has been traumatized ever since!"

"Since what? What did Riveria do to her?!"

"You missed out on the most important part!!"

"Ah, well, ya see, she tied her arms and legs to this handy lump of adamantite we had lyin' around, and then *sploosh*! Tossed her right in!"

"How was that supposed to teach her how to swim?!"

A few days after the matter at Meren was resolved, Loki had gathered Tione, Tiona, and Lefiya in the sitting room and was telling them all the story that explained why Aiz was so bad at swimming to this day.

Just then, Riveria, who happened to be passing by, popped her head through the open doorway.

"What's that, Aiz? Still can't swim? How about we have another one of our lessons, just like old times?"

"?!"

Aiz's whole body seized up in shock, and she began shivering uncontrollably.

FALL IN LOVE, GIRLS—I MEAN, WARRIORS

"No, no, no! The strongest male among them is that fine chienthrope man who bested us!"

"His bulging muscles, his piercing eyes, and his cute little tail!"

"Bullcrap! My werewolf man was way stronger than him! When I think of the way he looked down at me with those ruthless, amber eyes, I get the shivers!"

"That 'Ra-ool' boy was a lot stronger than he looked, too! Even though he was mostly just carrying weapons around, he looked so manly doing it!"

"Oh, I miss them already! All those strong, healthy males who gave us such a thrashing!"

Well, this is a terrifying sight.

That thought ran through Bache's mind as she gazed upon the scowling faces of her arguing sisters-in-arms.

"You're all wrong! No man can beat that hunky dwarf daddy who wiped the floor with us!"

"When his chunky fist met my nose…I think I fell in love!"

"I'll never forget his manly features as long as I live!"

After Tiona defeated her and halted the rite, Bache had woken up aboard the Amazonian ship docked in Port Meren. The world she woke up to, however, was completely different from the one she had left—or, more to the point, the people in it were.

"I want to be his mate!!"

"I want to have his children!!"

"It hurts...I can't stand being apart anymore..."

To be specific, they had all fallen helplessly in *lust* with the proud male warriors of *Loki Familia* who had thoroughly trounced them. Their cheeks were flushed, and the expressions on their faces were more akin to animals in heat than to brave Amazons.

It was a side effect, perhaps, of growing up on the island state of Telskyura. These women were forced to engage in endless battle, never learning the first thing about love, and so the moment they met a strong man, they fell for them, hard. The very same thing had happened to Tione, though, of course, Bache had no way of knowing about that.

What happened while I was out cold...? she thought, aghast. *I can't stop shaking. What am I seeing?*

As Tione had defeated her before she saw any of the men in action, Bache alone was spared the burden of her Amazonian instincts. Her sisters in battle were all weaker than her, and yet in this moment, Bache was utterly terrified of them.

And the worst of all was...

"...Haah..."

Argana sat by the window, hugging one leg and staring out over the waters of the lake. From time to time, she would let out a wistful sigh, softly tracing the bruise on her cheek with her finger before shaking her head to snap herself out of it and compose her slack-jawed face.

It was so embarrassing, Bache wanted to drop dead. "Kali, please, you have to do something..." she begged, turning to her goddess with tears in her eyes, but the child god wore only a blank stare.

"Our nation's finished..." she muttered.

A BOY AND A GIRL, RUNNING AHEAD
Animate Store Bonus

LOVE IS FELT IN THE BREAST(S)
GAMERS Store Bonus

ASKING HIM OUT?
Toranoana Store Bonus

AMAZONIAN THEATER
Melon Books Store Bonus

**LOVE LIFE ON LABYRINTH LANE:
A BEHIND-THE-SCENES STORY**
Sword Oratoria, Volume 7 Limited Edition

SWORD ORATORIA VOLUME 7

© Kiyotaka Haimura

A BOY AND A GIRL, RUNNING AHEAD

Orario was brimming with excitement for days after *Hestia Familia*'s success in the War Game. People raved tirelessly about how Bell beat the enemy commander in single combat, and it was impossible to walk down the street without hearing tales of his heroic exploits.

"Bell Cranell was so cool! You'd never guess it from how weak he looks!"

"That Little Rookie is impressive! Not bad for a rabbit boy!"

"So that Record Holder title ain't just for show, huh? And here I thought he was just a weedy little shrimp!"

Young and old, big and small, were united in their fervent enthusiasm for the boy no matter their race or gender.

All, that is, except for one girl…

"Grrr…!"

Lefiya couldn't stand hearing all this praise. She wasn't sure how to describe her feelings. Was it jealousy, frustration, anxiety? Or had Bell's heroic battle lit a fire in her heart, too? Whichever it was, one thing was for certain: Lefiya couldn't stop thinking about him.

Okay, maybe he was a teeny, tiny, little, teensy-weensy bit cool out there, but still! He had to rely on Aiz for everything, and she's not even in her familia! He's ill-bred, uncouth, shameless, and clueless about how to treat a woman! Um…what else…?

As if to counter all the praise she was hearing, Lefiya began mentally listing off every one of Bell's shortcomings she could think of.

As she walked through the street, her competitive nature burning a hole in her chest, she suddenly heard the boy's alias.

"Hey, Little Rookie! Where are you going?"

"!"

Lefiya looked up to see the white-haired boy running down the street.

"I'm off to the Dungeon with all my friends!" he called back.

"Well, good hunting to you! And take this!"

The shopkeeper tossed him an apple.

"Thank you!"

The white-haired boy caught it gratefully, clearly embarrassed at all the praise, and continued running toward the giant tower that stood at the city's center, jutting up into the clear blue sky.

That boy was always like that. Always running forward, braving the Dungeon, and chasing his dreams, his eyes set on the future, with nothing but a wish and a prayer.

"…Well, I can do that, too!"

With the sight burned freshly into her eyes, Lefiya set off running as well. She put her pointless fault finding aside and strove to light a fire in her heart once more.

She would never let him get one over on her. And with that resolve spurring her on, Lefiya headed for the Dungeon as well.

LOVE IS FELT IN THE BREAST(S)

A few days after Orario was revitalized by the excitement of the War Game, Tiona was walking down the street, minding her own business, when she spotted a familiar figure in the crowd.

It's Argonaut!

Before even calling out to him, she reflexively broke into a run, leaping onto the boy's back.

"Hey, Argonaut!!"

"Wah!!"

Naturally, Bell Cranell was taken aback. Tiona suddenly realized this was the sort of behavior she usually reserved for Aiz or Lefiya, but she quickly brushed those thoughts aside, focusing instead on Bell and the amazing feats she had recently seen. It was like she'd been shown a brand-new installment of those heroic tales she loved.

"You were so cool in the War Game, Argonaut! Well done! I was watching you in the magic mirror the whole time! I couldn't look away! Oh yeah, did Aiz bring you that bouquet of flowers we got you? I was supposed to be there, too, but I was busy that day, sorry!"

Still clinging to Bell's back, Tiona wrapped her legs around his torso and tousled his snow-white hair. People stopped and stared at the sight of this Amazonian girl acting like a complete monkey in the middle of the road.

"Even Finn and the others were impressed! They said—Hm? What's wrong?"

Tiona suddenly realized that while she had been going on and on,

Bell hadn't spoken a word. In fact, he was staring at the ground, his face bright red all the way to his ears.

"M-Ms....Tiona..." he muttered in an almost imperceptible voice. "You're...t-touching me...with your...erm..."

Tiona paused and looked down. Sure enough, her chest was pressed firmly against the back of the boy's head. She wasn't the most well-endowed girl in the world, but there was definitely something there.

The Amazonian girl peered up toward the sky. Countless memories of insults such as *"flattie"* and *"washboard"* ran through her head. She looked back down at the boy who seemed very conscious of her chest and suddenly got a big grin on her face.

"H-hey! M-Ms. Tiona? You're holding me even tighter now! D-didn't you hear me?!"

"......"

"Wh-why aren't you saying anything?! And why are you smiling like that?!"

"...Eh-heh-heh."

"N-no! P-please...Let me go—I'm begging youuuuuu!!"

Confused onlookers tilted their heads as the Amazon kept on rubbing her breasts against Bell's back.

ASKING HIM OUT?

A few days after *Hestia Familia*'s explosive performance in the War Game, Aiz trudged through the streets, carrying a bouquet of white flowers.

"I got the flowers Loki suggested," she muttered to herself. "I wonder if this'll be enough…"

Aiz was heading to the home of *Hestia Familia* to deliver her congratulations in person. She had personally trained Bell before the War Game, and now that training had evidently paid off.

"And there's…something else I need to ask him as well…"

Aiz shuffled the bouquet bashfully, blushing softly. To anyone who saw her, this awkward fidgeting could have meant only one thing: She was about to ask the boy she liked out on a date! Some gasped, some cheered, and some wept, but Aiz paid them no mind.

"I need to be brave…"

Steeling her nerve, Aiz quickened her step.

"Well done in the War Game," Aiz said. "And on getting more members, too. I'm really happy for you."

When Bell opened his front door to see Aiz standing there, he was swept away by a wave of happiness.

"Th-thank you so much, Ms. Aiz! You really shouldn't have!"

For the girl he admired to recognize and celebrate his achievements—it was almost more than Bell could bear. As he wrestled with his emotions, however, he noticed something.

Hm? Ms. Aiz? She's...fidgeting...

Indeed, she was. Her cheeks reddened, and her tender lips parted and closed, almost as though she wanted to say something.

C-could she be thinking...?

Bringing him flowers and standing on his doorstep, hesitating over how to proceed—a million young boys would only assume one thing. As soon as Bell realized what was coming, *poof*! Steam shot from his ears. *Calm down! That can't possibly be it!* his mind screamed, but his heart was having none of it. He could hear it already:

"You're so strong now. And handsome. Would you...?"

Bell gulped. And finally, Aiz worked up the courage to let it out.

"Would you...tell me how you managed to get to Level Three so quickly?"

"I should have known..."

Bell's voice croaked as his eyes welled with tears. There was only one thing on Aiz's mind at any given moment, and by now, Bell knew better than to expect that to change.

AMAZONIAN THEATER

"Hey, Tione."

"What?"

One afternoon, in a bedroom shared by a set of twins, one sister relaxed on the bed, while the other lay sprawled out over it.

"The others say they've been feeling watched lately."

"'Watched'? What on earth do they mean by that?"

"They've been getting chills, like someone's watching them, and if they let their guard down for even a minute, they'll be gobbled up, they say!"

"Hmph. It's probably some other familia, isn't it? Once we find out who they are, we should just march over there and crush them before they can do anything."

Tione flipped a page in her book, *Everything You Need to Know About Love!* Tiona turned over onto her back.

"Hey, Tione."

"What?"

"I heard some Amazons have been sneaking into Orario."

"Really? What about the Guild? Isn't it their job to keep them out?"

"I heard some of them smuggled themselves in wine barrels, and others just beat up the guards."

"That's so stupid; I can't believe it worked. Ganesha's people must be slacking off as well."

Tione began nibbling on her Jyaga Maru Kun. Tiona reached to tear a bit off, but her hand was batted away.

"Hey, Tione."

"What is it now?"

"I heard one of those Amazons is as strong as a snake."

"Hold on. Are you saying it's me, because my alias is the name of a snake?"

"No, no. It's someone else. I heard she came here searching for the man of her dreams."

"Disgusting. Just another Amazon who's thinking with her crotch instead of her head."

Tione angrily turned another page. Tiona stared at the ceiling.

"I heard that this Amazon said she'd never forget the way that prum man punched her."

"…"

Tione fell deathly silent. Tiona reached over and slipped the Jyaga Maru Kun from her hands.

"Hey, Tione."

"…What?"

"I forgot to say that Finn said one of those Amazons was following him around."

"Argana!!"

Consumed by a furious rage, Tione stormed out of the room, while Tiona munched happily on her new snack.

LOVE LIFE ON LABYRINTH LANE: A BEHIND-THE-SCENES STORY

"What about you, Aiz?"

It was the dead of night, and the girls of *Loki Familia* were gathered on Daedalus Street to search for the Dungeon's second entrance. The conversation, however, quickly turned to matters of love.

"There's...not really anybody I..."

"Come on, there must be *somebody*! Somebody you like just a little bit more than the rest, maybe?"

It all started when the group ran into Filvis during their investigations. The girl had a reputation for being a bit aloof, and so to break the ice, the conversation had somehow veered to this subject.

Filvis herself had already been bombarded with so many questions by this point that her head was spinning, and she was barely responding anymore. And so Tiona directed her eager questions at Aiz, while Lefiya strained her ears to listen, and the rest of the group all waited in hushed excitement for what Aiz would say.

Cornered and with no hope for rescue, Aiz hesitated for what seemed like ages. Then, at last, with no other choice, she opened her lips to answer.

"I..."

Then it happened. A boy's voice, unbearably embarrassed, caught the group's attention.

"U-um, I'm sorry! I wonder if you could help me?"

Hm? Don't I know that voice...?

The first to turn and look was Aiz. When she did, she spotted a source of light—a magic-stone torch—weaving its way through the darkness of the maze of streets toward them. The other girls all stared in confusion, and when the figure finally got close enough, Aiz could make out the stranger more clearly.

"I-I think I took a wrong turn somewhere..." he stammered. "D-do you ladies know the way out?"

A head of snow-white hair that lit up the night. A pair of rubellite eyes, now streaked with tears. It was almost like a little white rabbit had shuffled up to them.

"W-wait—it's you!"

When the young man saw their faces, he was even more taken aback than they were. Both parties stared in shock until Aiz broke the silence.

"...Bell?" she asked, and with that, time began flowing again.

"It's Argonaut!" cried Tiona. "But why?!"

"Wh-wh-wh-wh-what are you doing here?!" demanded Lefiya.

"L-Loki Familia?!" said the equally flustered boy. "A-and Ms. Aiz?!"

"Yeah...Good evening."

"G-good evening!!"

The two exchanged confused pleasantries, with Bell bowing deeply. There was no doubt now—the boy who had appeared on the street was none other than captain of *Hestia Familia* and hero of the recent War Game, Bell Cranell.

At length, Bell raised his head and scanned the stunned faces of *Loki Familia*.

"B-but what are you all doing out here so late at night?" he asked.

"Oh, er..." said Tione, hastily fabricating a lie to conceal the truth of their investigation from Bell. "What's that thing they do in the East? A test of courage! We're doing that!"

"A...'test of courage'?"

Bell didn't seem entirely convinced by this but raised no objection.

"What about you, then?" Tiona asked. "What are you doing around here?"

"Oh, er...!"

There was no mistaking it—when Tiona said that, Bell seized up. While the girls eyed him suspiciously, Tiona came over and sniffed.

"Hm? What's that smell on you, Argonaut? Are you wearing cologne?"

The animal people of the party all started sniffing, too. Aiz tried to follow suit, and when she did, she also detected a whiff of something unusual about the boy. It would have been strange for any man to be wearing perfume, let alone a country boy like Bell, and yet there it was, clear as day. A sweet, alluring, almost licentious scent.

"Oh, um...it's...er...!"

The boy was sweating buckets by now and couldn't seem to get out a single word. He refused to answer Tione's question, instead looking left and right as if searching for an escape route.

"Wait...I know that smell," said Aki, almost choking on the revelation.

Before she could say it, though, it was Filvis, silent up until now, who narrowed her eyes and muttered:

"Musk..."

Bell tensed his shoulders. Filvis shot him an ice-cold glare.

"B-by 'musk,' you mean...?" stammered the red-faced healer girl, Leene.

"Yes," said Aki. "The thing they use all the time in the Pleasure Quarter."

The Pleasure Quarter. Just the sound of its name silenced all the girls a second time.

...What?

Aiz was no exception. Slowly, she turned her golden eyes to the boy, who, even now, was dripping with sweat.

The Pleasure Quarter...? With all those...brothels?

The exact same moment Aiz's train of thought arrived at that word, Lefiya exploded.

"Th…that…That's IMMORAAAAAAAAAAAAL!!!"

Her face turned bright red as she screamed, "You were in the Pleasure Quarter?! Visiting a brothel?! So just a few moments ago, you were with a lady of the night?! Doing th-this and th-th-that and a-a-all sorts of other things?! Wraaaaaaaaaaaghhh!!"

"N-no!" Bell protested. "I can explain! I-I mean it! I really can!"

"What is there to explain?! And now that I get a closer look, that torch you're carrying was made in the Far-Eastern style! You really *were* at a brothel!"

Lefiya had all but lost her mind, pointing fingers and screeching accusations. Bell was faring little better, trying his best to explain the situation, but none of the girls were having any of it.

"Please, I'm begging you. Listen to me, Ms. Lefiya!"

"Never!! Don't even speak my name with that filthy tongue of yours! Only the gods know where it's been!"

"Gugh!"

"And I was just starting to think I was mistaken about you! I was just starting to think you put on a brave show during the War Game! Here I thought *maybe* you weren't the worst human being to ever walk this earth, but boy was I wrong!!!"

"Gagh!!"

"What an idiot I was to believe that, even for a second, you were anything more than a lecherous, womanizing, dirty little rabbit that's always in heat!!"

Bell was taking a serious verbal beating. Every curse from Lefiya made him double over like he'd been punched in the gut. By the time she was done, the elf girl was heaving with breath, tears in her eyes, and Filvis had to step between her and Bell to calm her down.

"Don't," she said. "Don't sully yourself. He's not worth it."

Filvis looked at Bell in the manner usually reserved for pieces of excrement lying by the side of the road. It was her words, delivered by an especially graceful member of the beautiful elf race, that finally left Bell coughing up blood.

"Ghah!!"

And even if they weren't quite as prudish as their elven comrades, the news of Bell's alleged misadventures still came as quite a shock to most of the other girls of *Loki Familia*. Some were aghast, some were repulsed, while others were just plain embarrassed.

Aiz, meanwhile, was dead silent. At first glance, it was the same unexpressive look as always, but behind her emotionless facade, her eyes were spinning.

A brothel…where men go…to be with women…and to do…mumble, mumble stuff…

Aiz was fairly naive on what, precisely, such an encounter normally entailed, but she understood the basic concept. And now, she felt like the boy had graduated from her "private" lessons (about combat, of course) and was steadily drifting away. It was as though she'd suddenly discovered a secret hobby of the boy next door she thought she knew…or more like if she'd followed her pet rabbit and found he had a secret nest with a family she had no idea about.

"I guess all guys have their needs, even Argonaut!" mused Tiona. "Hmm…that makes me a little bit sad for some reason."

"I'm telling you—you've got it all wrong, Ms. Tiona! I didn't do any—"

"It's okay! Amazons are like that, too! Well, most of us are! It's nothing to be ashamed of! Probably!"

"No, I…!"

"I won't judge," said Tione. "You do what you have to."

"I'm not doing anything like thaaat!"

In the end, even the two Amazons of the group were just as taken aback as the rest of them. Bell clutched his head, desperate to dispel the misunderstanding, while Aiz watched on in silence.

I can't...calm down.

Aiz's heart was racing fast. And just as she was trying to work out the reason why, Bell noticed her unbroken stare and turned to her.

"Oh..."

"...!"

When their eyes met, Aiz felt compelled to look anywhere else. She couldn't say why.

That, for Bell, was the most crushing blow of the night. The look on his face said the world was ending. Even the other girls recoiled at the sight of him.

"...Oh, right. We're heading back to the main road," said Tione, eager to take the focus off Bell's brutal public execution. "Would you like to come with us?"

"Yes, please..." said Bell, lacking the energy to raise his head or even give anything more substantial than a feeble nod.

And with that, the party set off anew, now with one more lost child among them.

"I really can't believe it! The nerve of that rabbit!"

"Hey, Lefiya, how come you're so angry with Argonaut anyway? When other people say and do stuff like that, you just get embarrassed."

"W-well, that's because he's my rival—I mean...I don't think he should get to play so fast and loose just because the fame he got from the War Game has gone to his head! It's obscene! If he wants Aiz to teach him—I mean...if he wants to be a proper adventurer, he should have a bit more grit and ambition!"

Lefiya was red-faced and raving, while an awkward gloom descended over the rest of the party. The cause, of course, was the dour-faced young boy in their midst. A dark cloud seemed to ooze from his very being, and Aiz, who was normally the first to jump to his defense at times like these, was oddly subdued. Bit by bit, a strange gulf of detachment was growing between Bell and the girls of *Loki Familia*.

"Erm…come to think of it, I wonder if any of our boys do that sort of thing," said Leene, frantically searching for another topic of discussion. "Do you think they've ever…erm…*visited* a prostitute?"

"You don't have to talk about it if it makes you blush so hard," replied Aki with a sigh. "But just for your information, Raul did use to go there quite often."

"What?!"

"Apparently, some conniving wench got the better of him," Aki went on. "You remember that time he stole all the money we made from our expedition? That was because he wanted to buy this woman a present."

"Oh, Raul…"

"But you know what he's like. He never got further than holding hands in the end…That silly boy, I don't know if he was trying to broaden his horizons or what, but he didn't have to go all the way to the Pleasure Quarter…"

As the entire group listened to Aki's story, the party's mood slowly transformed into a collective sigh at the shortcomings of the male species. Sensing the negativity take hold, Tiona attempted to lighten things up.

"Let's talk about something more fun!" she said. "I know! Let's go back to what we were talking about before!"

"What were you talking about before…?" asked Bell weakly.

"We were talking about if there were any boys we liked!" came Tiona's cheerful reply, causing Bell to look away once more and chew on his words. "And we were just about to hear what Aiz had to say, weren't we?" she added, jumping on the girl's back.

"…!"

Bell snapped to attention. He suddenly started acting very oddly indeed, still trying to distance himself from the conversation but sneaking frequent glances in Aiz's direction.

The other girls all simultaneously thought, *Oh yeah, that is what we were talking about*, and turned to Aiz expectantly.

"Come on, Aiz!" Tiona urged her. "What guy do you like?"

"I...um..."

Her eyes darted around for a way out, but eventually, Aiz's stare fell on Bell, and she opened her lips to speak.

"There...isn't really anybody I like..."

"...But...?" asked Tiona, sensing she still had something to say.

"...I don't think I like...men who fool around."

Stab!!

Everyone swore they could hear the knife that pierced Bell's heart at that moment. They turned to see him clutching his chest.

"Or...men who go to the Pleasure Quarter..."

"Aghh!"

"Or men who smell like musk."

"Guhh!!"

"I hate that."

"Ghah!!"

Aiz didn't so much as glance in Bell's direction. She simply rattled off a list of misgivings that nearly folded the poor boy in half. It was clearly a hundred times worse hearing it from Aiz's lips than it had been from Lefiya's. Speaking of whom...

"I'm so glad to see we're in agreement, Ms. Aiz! You really can't trust the types of men who frequent those sorts of places!"

"...Yeah." Aiz nodded. Meanwhile, the whole group was abuzz, with people turning to one another and muttering:

"What a strong opinion!"

"I've never heard Aiz talk for so long!"

"She must really hate those men!"

Tione and Aki grinned awkwardly. They weren't sure what to make of this side of Aiz. Filvis, meanwhile, had her eyes closed like she wanted nothing to do with any of it.

And Bell...

"U...urgh..."

The boy weakly collapsed against the wall at the side of the street.

He looked like he was about to be sick or like his soul were trying to leave his body.

"Hmm..."

Tiona glanced first at the boy's sad state and then at the lonely-looking Aiz. She climbed off the girl's back and jogged over to the back of the group, where Bell was hanging his head in shame.

"Hey, Argonaut?" she asked.

"Yeah...?"

"Did you really not do anything while you were there?"

Bell's response was instant. "Absolutely not! I really didn't! I didn't do anything—I swear!!"

"You swear to the gods?"

"I swear to my goddess!"

"Hmm..."

Tiona crossed her arms and pondered. If Bell was willing to go that far to proclaim his innocence, then it was really hard to imagine he wasn't telling the truth.

"But you were definitely there, weren't you?" she asked. "So why?"

"Well, a new member of our familia went off by herself to the Pleasure Quarter, and we got worried. Welf...erm, my friends came with me to look for her, but I got separated..."

"Then why do you smell like musk?"

"Erm...well, one of the, er, Amazon ladies...kind of, er, abducted me..."

"Huh?"

Tiona's eyes went wide.

"You mean, one of the prostitutes took you back to the brothel?"

"...Y-yeah..."

"A-are you okay?! Did they do anything to you?!"

Tiona was an exception, but by and large, Amazons were aggressive lovers. If a male caught their attention, they wouldn't just sit back and wait for him to come to them—they'd take the initiative. Even Tione possessed something of this aggressive nature—though only when pursuing Finn, of course. Tiona was starting to wonder if the boy had been robbed of his innocence out there, especially once he looked up with sad, empty eyes.

"I'm okay, but…"

"B-but?"

"Women are scary women are scary Amazons are scary Amazons are scary—frogs are scary!"

Bell immediately hugged himself and shivered violently. What kind of desperate escape was he remembering? His complete mental breakdown caused Tiona to take a step back.

"Oh man…"

It seemed her fellow Amazons had given the boy a truly difficult time. Still, that was all Tiona needed to hear. She was sure the boy was telling the truth now.

"It's okay, Argonaut. I believe you."

"…Really?"

"I might not know a lot, but I know you're not lying."

Not after that embarrassing display, she tactfully omitted, and she shot Bell a sunny smile.

"Leave it to me," she said. "I'll explain to Aiz and the other girls that they've all got the wrong idea!"

"M-Ms. Tiona…!"

"Heh-heh! Just wait right here!"

Tiona left Bell, who was crying tears of gratitude, and set off to rejoin the rest of her party. There was a spring in her step, thinking how happy she was for Bell to be thanking her. She liked Aiz, and though she hadn't known him for very long, she liked Bell as well. She couldn't just watch on as two people she cared about fell out over some silly misunderstanding. She had to step in and do something.

"Aiz! Argonaut says he didn't do anything at the Pleasure Quarter!"

"…What?"

"He was there for a good reason!"

Tiona decided to clear up the misunderstanding with Aiz first. Reattaching herself to Aiz's back, she explained all she'd heard to the confused-looking girl.

"An Amazon...abducted him? And chased him around the district?"

"The Pleasure Quarter's where the Berbera of *Ishtar Familia* hang out," said Tiona. "I bet they all had their eyes on him after he got famous because of the War Game."

"..."

After listening to Tiona's explanation, Aiz fell into silent thought. Her eyes flickered over to the far rear of the group, where Bell was walking, awaiting judgment like a sentenced criminal.

"Tiona, I think I need to..."

"Yep! Go ahead!"

Aiz excused herself and slowed her pace so that the whole party overtook her, and she ended up walking side by side with Bell, at the very back.

"A-Aiz..."

"..."

Bell awkwardly froze upon seeing her. Aiz didn't fare much better and hurriedly tried to think of something to say. Her eyes darted from side to side as the gears turned, and then finally, she parted her lips to speak.

"I heard..." she said, "from Tiona...Did that really happen?"

"Y-yes!"

Aiz studied the boy's rubellite eyes for any trace of deception, but in the end, she came to the same conclusion that Tiona had. The uneasy feeling in her heart disappeared, washed away by a wave of relief...immediately followed by the utmost shame.

"Um...I, er..." she muttered.

"Hm?"

"I'm...sorry I doubted you..." she said, sadly looking down at her feet. She couldn't believe she'd jumped to conclusions without even listening to Bell's side of the story.

Wide-eyed, Bell waved his hands.

"N-no, no, no! I don't blame you at all! In fact, I'm surprised you believed me in the end! P-please don't feel bad about it!"

"...Thank you..."

Even when he was the one under attack, Bell always put others first. That only made Aiz feel even guiltier, but a faint, almost imperceptible smile appeared on her lips and in the corners of her eyes. Recognizing it for what it was, Bell blushed.

"Did anything bad happen to you?" Aiz asked.

"N-no, I'm fine...mostly."

"That's good..."

"E-erm?"

Aiz ran her fingers through his hair. Bell went bright red and tried to pull away, but she didn't stop stroking his snow-white head.

A little white rabbit that ran away from home had finally returned to its master's care.

Aiz smiled, daydreaming about picking up that small animal and rubbing its fur against her cheek.

And Bell, relieved beyond belief, smiled back.

"Mrrrgh...!"

Meanwhile, Lefiya grumbled to herself as she watched the pair.

Tiona was still going around the group, clearing up the misunderstanding, but Lefiya had already heard, and her heart was heavy with guilt.

Grr, I said all those terrible things. Maybe I should apologize...but it's his *fault for being so vulgar that I* could *believe it! ...But I suppose I should have listened to his side of the story...Oh, darn it!*

As she wrestled with the disparity between her preconceptions and the truth, Lefiya slowly realized that she needed to say something, so she headed over to where Bell was walking. Watching her handle her emotions maturely, Filvis gave a small, unseen smile and followed behind to offer her own apologies to the boy.

"E-excuse me!"

"Oh, Ms. Lefiya..." said Bell, pausing his conversation with Aiz and turning to face her.

"Um...I, er...I have something to say!"

Lefiya faltered, unable to meet his gaze. But just as she began to speak, something clattered after falling from Bell's waist pouch.

"...Hm? What's this...?"

It was a small vial about the shape and size of a chess piece, filled with a brilliant red liquid. Lefiya bent down to pick it up, but before she could even get a good look, Bell swiped it away at the speed of sound and hid it behind his back.

"Oh, that? That's just a little...something...Ah-ha-ha-ha-ha..."

Lefiya studied his awkward smile. He was acting very suspiciously indeed. It didn't take a genius to know he was hiding something. Lefiya's eyebrows furrowed.

"What was that thing you were trying to hide?" she demanded.

"Oh, er...don't worry about that. Somebody, er...gave it to me, or...forced it on me...it's, er...really not that important!"

Bell was sweating waterfalls and making little sense, which only reinforced the notion that it was something Lefiya ought to know. But just as she was about to press Bell for details, Filvis spoke up in a flat tone.

"That was a virility potion..."

The air froze. Time stopped. Everyone—Aiz, Lefiya, every girl within earshot, and even Tiona, busy defending—went silent. A single bead of sweat worked its way down Bell's pallid cheek.

Filvis's second bombshell of the night had brought all the panic of the musk fiasco right back.

"Wh-whaaaaat?!"

Lefiya exploded.

"A v-v-v-virility potion?! Why on earth do you have that? I thought you said you didn't do anything!!"

"I didn't, I didn't, I didn't! I mean, I did do *something*, obviously, but I didn't do anything!!"

"You're not making any sense whatsoever! Hand that over and let me see it!!"

"W-wait, Lefiya! You've got it all wrong!"

Ignoring the boy's panicked cries, Lefiya marched straight over to him and tried to wrest the potion from his grip. A struggle ensued, and the two struggled for control of the vial before...

"Uh-oh."

With a mighty tug from Lefiya, the glass bottle flew out of Bell's hands. The stopper worked itself free and, as if ordained by fate, the uncorked vial sailed gracefully through the air before landing on Lefiya's head and spilling its contents all over her hair.

"Oh..."

Bell paled. Aiz couldn't speak. Filvis froze. Tiona, Tione, and all the other girls stood in shock, mouths agape.

"..."

Lefiya's arms dropped limply. The scarlet potion seeped into her amber hair and beautiful skin, giving rise to a strange odor not at all fitting for a modest young elf girl.

A dark cloud descended over her, robbing the light from her eyes.

"I...I..."

She shivered, unable to speak a word. Then, all at once, she unleashed the grandest explosion of the night.

"I hate men like youuuuuuuuuuuuuuuuuuuuu!!"

"I'm sorryyyyyyyyyyyyyyyyyyyyyyyyyyyyyyyyy!!"

Bell swiped the empty vial off the ground and scampered away like a startled rabbit, and Lefiya took off after him.

"L-Lefiya!"

"Argonaut?!"

Aiz's and Tiona's shouts did not reach them. Tione, Filvis, and the other girls watched on blankly as a gust of wind swept past them, and the boy and the girl vanished into the darkness of the mazelike streets.

Aiz's group quickly abandoned any hopes of regrouping with Loki's party and instead turned their efforts toward searching for the missing Bell and Lefiya.

It was dawn of the following day when they finally came across a single elf girl, sobbing by the side of the road, sad and alone after failing to catch the white rabbit.

Watching the girl cry into Riveria's breast, Loki muttered, "What the heck's eatin' her...?"

Lefiya refused to speak about what had transpired, and Aiz and the other girls all averted their gazes when questioned. The high elf simply stroked the girl's amber hair and sighed.

And due to the scars suffered by one young girl, *Loki Familia* withdrew from Daedalus Street and returned home.

"Phew...I think I got away...I'm so sorry about that, Ms. Lefiya..."

Meanwhile, battered and exhausted, one adventurer boy crawled out of Orario's tangled backstreets. He had been running all night, and as the morning light scorched his eyes, he cursed his rotten luck.

However, the worst was yet to come.

For, unbeknownst to him, someone was watching him leave the shadowy back alleys. A goddess who had grown worried about his prolonged absence had come to look for him. Bell failed to notice her watchful gaze, which turned scornful the moment she smelled the musk on him and saw the half-empty vial of aphrodisiac in his hands.

Bell was forced to kneel silently and listen to her complaints for the rest of the day.

Why did I bring that bottle with me...?

The next day, Bell kneeled before an uneasy Aiz and a mentally scarred Lefiya to explain the situation and beg their forgiveness.

GUILTY!!

"Oh dear, I took much longer than I was supposed to! I'm sure everyone else has already met up…!"

Lefiya jogged through the streets after questioning the Amazons. The whole familia was out in full force searching for clues about Knossos, and as it was already noon, it was time to gather and discuss what they'd learned. While Lefiya was on her way to the rendezvous point, however, a curious sight made her screech to a halt.

"Hm?!"

She spotted, from behind, a white-haired man walking alongside a blond-haired girl.

It's that human! And he's with Aiz again! Doesn't he know to stick to his own familia?!

Completely forgetting her mission, she cried out, "Hey!" and ran over to the couple.

"Wah! M-Ms. Lefiya?"

"I can't believe you! Haven't you learned your lesson? What are you doing out here, cavorting around with…Aiz? Huh?"

When she turned, Lefiya realized the blond-haired woman with Bell was not Aiz at all—it was a renart girl she'd never seen before. She was wearing some kind of maid outfit that had eluded Lefiya at a distance, and the two of them were carrying bags as though they'd just been shopping together.

"'Aiz'?" repeated Bell. "No, no, this is someone who recently joined our familia!"

"P-pleased to meet you," said the renart girl, meekly bowing her head.

Lefiya went bright red, as she realized the only reason she had intervened was because her mind had seen white hair and blond hair and automatically put two and two together.

Ohh, what a gaffe! But how was I supposed to know? From behind, she looks exactly...the...same...?

Lefiya's internal monologue slowed to a crawl, for when she looked up at the renart girl, she noticed something. The girl was incredibly pretty. Not as pretty as Aiz, of course—or rather, she was pretty in different ways, and it didn't make sense to compare—but in any case, Lefiya found herself dumbstruck by the girl's beauty.

Her golden hair reminded her of Aiz's, and her features were no less fair. For Bell to be seen with such a girl...wasn't that effectively a form of adultery?

A few moments later, Lefiya's emotions boiled over and she exploded.

"H-h-h-h-how can you betray Aiz like this, you cheat?!"

"'Ch-cheat'? B-but I'm not even going out with Aiz!"

"Of course you aren't! But that doesn't mean you can leave her in the dirt and go strutting around town with someone else!!"

"What do you meeean?!"

"B-Bell's m-m-mistress? Ohh..."

As an elf and a human began arguing in the street, one renart girl fainted, much to the confusion of passersby.

WELL, I DIDN'T THINK IT WAS POSSIBLE...

"*Don't let it get in the way of your work, but do you think you could keep an eye out for Bete?*"

Just as Aiz had been getting ready to comb the city for clues on Knossos, Loki came to her with a request. After Bete clashed with some of the girls in the familia, he had promptly stormed off. Aiz wasn't particularly concerned, but when Loki said, "*You're the only one I can count on for this,*" the little girl inside Aiz's mind was filled with proud determination. It was almost like she was a secret agent on a mission for her boss.

First, I should check out all of Bete's usual hangouts...

Exiting the mansion, Aiz began her search. Recalling that Loki had suggested asking Lefiya for help if she needed it, Aiz sought out the elf to hear her advice.

"Ah, Lefiya, there you are," said Aiz, spotting her in the street. "I was just wondering if..."

"L-l-listen to this, Ms. Aiz!!"

Lefiya came running up, a frightful look on her face.

"I heard from Elfie that Bete's on a date with a girl from another familia!!" she cried.

"...?"

After a long, drawn-out silence, Aiz tilted her head.

"Lefiya...? Are you sure you're feeling all right?" she asked, a bleak look in her stoic eyes.

"Please don't look at me like that! I'm not crazy—I swear! Elfie said when she saw him on the north side, she was so shocked she couldn't stand up straight!!"

Aiz turned and contented herself with the explanation that Lefiya must have been exhausted and surely not thinking straight. "So he's in the north? Thanks, Lefiya," she said, and began marching off, ignoring the elf girl's cries of "I'm serious! Why don't you believe me?!"

Bete on a date...Can't imagine that.

The little girl in her mind, now wearing a black suit and tie, agreed, shaking her arms in denial, saying *No, no, no!*

Practically the first thing out of Bete's mouth in any situation was "I hate weak women," so it was difficult—nay, impossible—to imagine him fooling around with girls. Bete had been a part of Aiz's familia long enough by now that she was sure of it. Aiz was so confident that even she made that declaration.

"If he really is on a date..." she said to herself. "I'll stand on my head and eat my hat."

Thirty minutes later, Aiz was begging for forgiveness, and the little girl inside her mind was doing precisely that.

SECRETS OF THE DATE

"Here, Bete Loga, open wide!"

I'm going to murder you.

Bete looked at the smiling Amazon and the spoonful of cake in her hand, and his eyes were filled with murderous rage. He and Lena were sitting outside a small café off North Main Street, where they had stopped after their Dungeon date to fill their bellies. If Bete had known this was coming, he would have refused—and according to the cheerful Amazon, she still intended to go shopping together after this as well!

But before that, Bete had to overcome the daunting task before him: the infamous *"open wide."*

Bete knew all about this humiliating ritual thanks to all the times Loki had tried to force it on Aiz and the other girls in the familia. Merely hearing its name made his blood boil.

"Aren't you hungry, Bete Loga?" asked Lena in a singsong voice. "If you don't eat, I'll be so sad I might forget all about the key you wanted to know about!"

Bete's lips warped into a twisted scowl. "You little...!"

Meanwhile, Lena simply giggled. Bete couldn't refuse. Not if he wanted to learn more about Knossos. Lena left him no choice but to swallow his pride...along with the contents of her spoon.

Dammit! Guess I have to get it over with before anyone sees...!

At least wanting to go out on his own terms, Bete grabbed Lena's hand and pulled the offering toward his mouth.

"Wow! Easy there, tiger!"

However, like a trick played by fate, a single white-haired young boy picked that exact moment to turn the corner.

"...Huh?"

Bell was stupefied, and Bete's jaw hit the floor, while Lena turned and cheerfully said, "Oh, look, it's Little Rookie!"

Bete went fiery red to the very tips of his ears.

"I...I'm sorryyyyyyyyyyyyyyyyyyyyy!"

"Hey! Come back here! You didn't see a damn thing, got it?!!"

Bete got out of his seat and chased after the fleeing Bell, returning only after extracting a promise of absolute confidentiality.

NOT GOOD-BYE, BUT THANK YOU

At the end of it all, there was one memory that occupied Leene's mind.

"I'm still just as weak as you say. But I can help keep you safe out there. Will you...let me come with you?"

That was what Leene had said as she had taken his hand and enveloped the battered young werewolf in a healing light. Bete had paused for a long moment before he answered.

"Do what you want. If you think you can keep up, then just try it."

Leene had been overjoyed to hear that. His answer made her spirit soar and filled her heart with warmth. She hoped that one day, she would be able to mend all the scars in his heart, even the deepest ones...

...That wish would have to stay unfulfilled.

"You and the others died for nothing. You died 'cause you were weak and stupid, and now you're gonna carry that shame for what's left of your miserable lives and into the next one."

The stone walls of Knossos were bathed in the blood of her friends. Leene lay there alone dying, listening to Bete's scornful words. She knew what he was telling her to do. She knew he was upholding his duty, the responsibility of the strong to the weak.

And he was strong. For all his scars, Bete was the strongest wolf she had ever known.

I ended up hurting him. That goes against the cardinal rule that every healer follows.

The guilt was enough to drive her mad. She really was every bit as weak as Bete said.

"Well, get it over with. Don't let me see you in the next life. Don't even leave your nest if you know what's good for you."

The sound faded. The world seemed to grow smaller. Inescapable death was near. Through it all, she never took her eyes off him. Though she lacked the strength to talk, her eyes communicated her final regret and asked for forgiveness.

"You dumbass."

And then he spoke his final words to her.

"How many times have your hands saved me? You've done enough."

Leene's eyes flew open, and tears began to fall.

When she closed her eyes for the last time, she wore a peaceful smile on her lips, and her heart rested easy now that she knew her efforts had not been in vain. A warm feeling enveloped her, bringing solace in her final moments, as Leene's soul softly slipped from this world.

Her very last thought was *I'm so glad I fell in love with him.*

AFTER RETURNING HOME
Animate Store Bonus

AFTERWARD: THE GIRL AND THE WOLF
GAMERS Store Bonus

ESSENCE OF A PARENT
Toranoana Store Bonus

RECOLLECTION OF A BLACKSMITH
Melon Books Store Bonus

SWORD ORATORIA VOLUME 9

© Kiyotaka Haimura

AFTER RETURNING HOME

"I'm back, Riveria."

"Ah, welcome back, Aiz."

Aiz and Riveria exchanged pleasant smiles while the rest of the familia looked on happily. Aiz had just returned from her trip to Edas Village. Beneath the warm sun, Aiz said her sorries and thank-yous as a gentle, heartwarming mood descended over the crowd.

...Until Lefiya, with an altogether different look in her eyes, stepped up to Aiz.

"So tell me," she said. "I heard th-th-that human boy from *Hestia Familia* was there as well. H-h-how did you spend those five days?"

"...Hm?"

"You know! Deep in the mountains, with no refuge...D-d-d-don't tell me you had to seek shelter from the rain in a cave somewhere and s-s-strip down and p-p-press your bodies together for warmth?!?!"

Lefiya didn't know about Edas Village, and as a result, she had clearly succumbed to delusion. While Tiona, Bete, and the others present looked on in shock, she demanded to know exactly what her beloved swordswoman had gotten up to with that despicable knave.

"I-I just mean," said Lefiya, switching tack, "he didn't try anything weird with you, did he?"

At the mention of the word "weird," Aiz recalled something. A memory of trying to get Bell to open up. His refusal, her offense, pushing him over, knocking him down...As soon as she remembered, her cheeks flushed in shame, and she began fidgeting awkwardly.

Lefiya and the rest of the team couldn't believe what they were seeing.

"M-Ms. Aiz?! Don't tell me he really *did* do something?!"

"N-no…It's more like…I…did something to him…"

"What?!"

"I grabbed Bell…and pushed him onto the bed…"

""""Wh-whaaaaaaaaaaaat?!""""

The entire familia cried out in unison. Lefiya and the rest of Aiz's groupies fainted on the spot. The Hyrute twins suddenly got all excited, and even Bete froze in shock. It was utter chaos.

"You foolish girl…You really are a handful."

Only Riveria, who knew how airheaded Aiz could be, managed to deduce what had really happened and rubbed the bridge of her nose in exasperation.

AFTERWARD: THE GIRL AND THE WOLF

"Ohh, you're so rough, Bete Loga! Dragging me along with no explanation! Mm, but I like that forceful side of you!"

"Shut up, you stupid kid!"

The sun had set, the full moon shone high in the sky, and the voices of an Amazon and a werewolf echoed through the streets of the Pleasure Quarter undergoing reconstruction in the southwest of the city. The girls of *Loki Familia* followed alongside them.

It was the fifth night after the Kingdom of Rakia attacked the Labyrinth City, and *Loki Familia* had chosen to retreat, but Bete decided to bring Lena Tully with him. This was because the issue of how to get into Knossos had not yet been resolved, and Lena was the key to unlocking it all. Right now, the group was heading to Belit Babili, where Lena claimed to have spotted something that would help.

However, Tiona and Tione were making heckling comments from the back of the group.

"Keep it down, Bete, or Guild security is going to figure out we're here!"

"Is it just me, or is he enjoying it?"

"Why don't you two just get married already? She's a little weird, but she's the best you're going to get!"

"Yeah, you'll be lucky if you ever find anyone weird enough to fall in love with you after her and Leene!"

"Thank you, sisters! Rest assured that I shall marry Bete Loga one day!"

"Shut up, you lousy Amazons, before I kick your heads off!"

Unable to take any more of this, Bete ran ahead, leaving the whole group behind except Lena, who managed to catch up to him. Once the two were alone, the Amazon's playful nature went away. She leaned against Bete and whispered with a faint smile on her lips.

"Hey, Bete Loga."

"What?"

"Thank you for the flowers."

Bete's ears twitched.

"I'm so happy you remembered."

"Shut up."

"When I saw them there, I wanted to cry."

"Shut up."

"Thank you. I love you."

"…Shut up."

ESSENCE OF A PARENT

"Riveria's really grown as a mother these past few years."

"...Must you keep saying that, Loki? Do not try my patience."

"Ha-ha-ha! The fact you no longer deny the matter so harshly means there must be some grain of truth to it!"

Loki, Riveria, and Gareth were gathered in the familia study, enjoying a pleasant conversation on a sunny afternoon. Currently, the conversation centered around Riveria, who had been recalling stories from Aiz's childhood as of late.

"Ya must be feelin' lonely now that you don't have to take care of her no more!"

"Perish the thought. What I want for the child more than anything is for her to grow up healthy and be happy."

"Hmph! You may say that, but we all know very well that you'll change your tune once she finds herself a man!"

"Gareth, you loon! I'll let no two-bit, stinkin' man lay his hands on my little angel! She's gonna live here with me in peace and happiness forever!"

"Now why are *you* getting angry...?"

Loki panted and panted, before turning her attention back to the important matter—making fun of Riveria. "But I see what you mean," she said. "If Aiz really did get a boyfriend—and I ain't sayin' she will—I bet Riveria here wouldn't shut up about him! She'd be like, 'You think you're worthy of my daughter?!' Hee-hee-hee!"

"Well, of course I would."

All of a sudden, Riveria's tone completely changed.

"Any potential suitor must be thoroughly vetted by me personally. I won't stand for any mangy hound dragged in off the street, you know. Oh, no. He must be an intellectual and dignified, too. Not to elf standards, of course. I'm not a tyrant, but he must have a modicum of sense and decorum. Any less would be simply unacceptable, I'm afraid. Next, while I know this sounds strict, he should be capable enough to protect Aiz should the need ever arise. Put simply, he should be strong enough to defeat me—or so I would have said if I were several centuries younger. Unfortunately, such practices have fallen out of vogue recently, but at the very least, he must be Aiz's equal. As for race, well, let's leave that up to her. As long as he's someone Aiz truly loves, then I'll accept anyone—yes, even a dwarf. However, if a god gets involved with her, then I'm afraid I'll have to step in. Aiz is deeply connected to the spirits, and I refuse to have anyone come barging into her life only to dredge up old wounds and..."

...*Aw crap, she isn't just her momma—she's her daddy, too!*

Elves are such a bothersome bunch...

Loki and Gareth both wore vacant stares as there was no end in sight to Riveria's tirade.

RECOLLECTION OF A BLACKSMITH

Oh, that won't survive long.

Such were Tsubaki's thoughts when she saw Aiz for the first time.

It was before she had even heard about the girl from Gareth. At that time, Tsubaki didn't know who Aiz was. She had just descended into the upper levels of the Dungeon to break in a new weapon she'd forged when she spotted Aiz turning a horde of monsters into mincemeat. Blood had stained her face, cuts and bruises had marred her fair skin, and the eyes of her doll-like face had been burned with what seemed like black fire. To a smith like Tsubaki, the girl looked like a sword—no different from one of the many lifeless killing tools her forge produced. The girl had seen herself as a weapon, a blade to be abused until it broke. How long could a blade last under those conditions? That was the first thing Tsubaki thought.

And that was why her first words to the girl were *"If you want to break a sword, why not try the one in your hands first?"*

However, the next time Tsubaki saw the girl, she noticed something different.

Oh?

Aiz still spent her days ruthlessly slaughtering monsters. She still saw herself as nothing more than a sword. Only now, she was not nearly as reckless as before. It was a subtle change, but to Tsubaki's one good eye, it was a noticeable one.

When the battle was over, Aiz waddled over to her high-elf

guardian and meekly allowed her blood-soaked face to be washed. It was an expression Tsubaki never expected to see the Doll Princess make.

"...Erm, excuse me..."

Then a few days later in Tsubaki's workshop, they met again. At Gareth's urging, Tsubaki presumed.

"Hm? Back again? I told you I ain't makin' you a weapon."

However, the golden-haired, golden-eyed girl shook her head.

"I don't want...a sword," she said. "I want...a hairpin."

Aiz stared at the ground, her cheeks softly reddening.

"...Is it for somebody?" Tsubaki asked.

"N-no...It's for me..." replied Aiz in a feeble voice. "My hair's getting longer...and it's getting in the way..."

Tsubaki smiled. "Very well," she said. "I'll make it. I won't ask for payment, either; you've got me interested now."

Aiz was surprised to hear that, but Tsubaki immediately set about crafting the ornament in her spare time. She pictured something that would pair well with the jade-green hair of the girl's high-elf guardian, when the two were seen standing side by side from the back.

Maybe that sword wasn't about to break after all.

Maybe one day, that sword would find its sheath.

And maybe, just maybe, the girl was changing. The blacksmith smiled and returned her focus to her work.

SWORD ORATORIA VOLUME 10

AND SO THE GIRL SETS OFF RUNNING ONCE MORE
First Printing

© Kiyotaka Haimura

AND SO THE GIRL SETS OFF RUNNING ONCE MORE

The following events took place after *Loki Familia* withdrew from Knossos and shortly after Finn's negotiations with Fels and the Xenos on the twelfth floor of the Dungeon.

Nobody spoke a word about how it all made them feel—about the idea of making deals with monsters, even intelligent ones. But as everyone trudged along in contemplative silence, Lefiya suddenly lifted her head.

Something was about to happen. She could feel it.

Reemerging onto the beaten path, *Loki Familia* came face-to-face with a mangled, scattered mess of monster corpses, as if a black wind had passed through. The corpses formed a trail, leading upward, a path of gore so vivid and distinct that Lefiya swore she could hear in her ears the distant roar of a mad bull.

Something had come through here, on its way up to the surface.

What would become of the boy that *something* had once fought?

At once, Lefiya started running.

"Lefiya! Where are you going?"

"I'm sorry! I've got to reach the surface, right now!"

It was on the ninth floor that Lefiya's patience finally gave out, and she parted from her comrades. With Riveria's voice ringing in her ears, she ran and ran, hoping against hope she wouldn't come across any of the boy's possessions—or body parts—that made up the trail of destruction she followed. Lefiya shook her head to rid herself of these intrusive thoughts and hurried on. By some miracle, the monsters seemed too terrified to even come near the beast's wake, and she reached the first floor without encountering any resistance at all.

"………"

When she did, she couldn't believe her eyes. There was an enormous crater replacing the path leading from the Dungeon entrance, the trail known as Beginning Road. It looked as if a small meteor had struck the earth, and although the Dungeon had already begun to regenerate, it was far from complete. Worried, Lefiya stepped across the cracked ground and made her way to the center of the crater, which was completely empty. There was no one there, just stones and broken magic torches from Babel littering the floor. Lefiya looked up to see a partially destroyed spiral staircase and a faint light.

She set off running once more. She hopped up the fragments of the staircase, into the lowest floor of Babel, past the confused *Ganesha Familia* guard, and up toward the surface, where she saw…

"Oh no…"

A massive hole had been blown in the side of the wall. It was the first floor of Babel, but even the large stained glass flower in the floor was barely recognizable.

Instead, many healers swarmed the halls, a half-elf had fallen to her knees, and one boy comforted her, holding her hand.

"We have enough healers now! Bring more stretchers!"

"The one who's been treated with Jewel Gel has a severe spine injury!"

"We can't lose an adventurer who fought so hard, no matter how foolish he is!"

Lefiya almost couldn't hear the frantic cries of the healers at that moment. The only thing reflected in her azure irises was the boy and the poor half-elf girl at his feet.

His white hair was slick with blood, hiding his rubellite eyes, but

Lefiya could see the teardrops rolling down his cheeks as he sobbed hoarsely, his throat and chest quivering.

They were tears of bitter regret. Tears Lefiya had never seen him shed. She had never seen him weep so openly or so violently despite all the pain and hardship he had endured.

She was shocked. Her voice refused to come out. All she felt was anger—an anger she couldn't tell came from envy.

He's going to keep growing.

The boy would weather this defeat and grow stronger than ever before.

He's going to get past this and keep growing.

This would be a turning point for him. A moment to slip the bonds of his past self.

Her faith was so strong, she almost seemed like an oracle. Lefiya clenched her fingers around her staff and steeled her resolve once more.

"You won't beat me."

There was only one worthy of being Bell's rival, and that was her. There was no need for pity or helping hands. She would have spurned any if the roles were reversed. With that solemn vow engraved upon her heart, Lefiya turned away and ran.

She would not lose to him, either.

MEMORY OF DAYS LOST

"Ya got a minute, Fil-Fil?"

It was more than two months prior when *Loki Familia* first stood before the gates of Knossos, ready to set foot in the man-made labyrinth, when Loki approached Filvis with a question.

"I'm glad you're helpin' us out on this mission," she said with her usual smile. "But where's that hoity-toity god o' yours?"

"If you are referring to Lord Dionysus, he is not here," Filvis replied. "I am carrying out his orders to provide you with assistance."

Filvis's words, however, were not the truth. Dionysus had told her nothing of the sort. Filvis was there on her own initiative for a very specific reason.

"Hmm..." Loki mused. "All right, then, one more question." She opened one eye just a crack. "Is Dionysus tryna hide somethin' from us?"

Filvis shuddered. The keen, probing gaze of *Loki Familia*'s goddess sent a shiver down her spine. But her unrest lasted only a moment. The next instant, she calmly closed her eyes and assumed total silence. That was the only way to keep secrets from a divine interrogator who could see through any lie.

Although gods could detect falsehoods, they lacked the power to read people's minds. Filvis knew all about her god's misfortune in the heavens but couldn't speak to Loki about it for fear of turning her suspicions against him. And so she summoned her sole defense: silence.

Loki shrugged and sighed, and suddenly the intense, interrogative mood lifted. She opened both eyes fully.

"Let me ask one last question, then," she said. "Why do you care so much about our Lefiya?"

This time, Filvis's answer was immediate.

"Because I wish to protect her."

There was no lie in those words. Filvis Challia was intent on keeping Lefiya Viridis alive. An inexplicable compassion moved her to do so—a feeling so strong that it drove her to defy even her patron god's command.

Lefiya didn't know. When she had called Filvis beautiful, she hadn't known how much that meant to her. She didn't know how much her honest words had changed Filvis's thoughts, changed her very self.

Filvis loved her. She loved that kindhearted girl as a true friend and sister-in-arms. That love was who she truly was, and no one could take that away.

Despite lacking her omniscience, perhaps Loki discerned that truth after all, for the goddess allowed Filvis to rejoin the party.

"You're her knight in shinin' armor, ain'tcha?"

Filvis's only reaction was to blush and quickly walk off.

"..."

Why was it that she remembered those words now?

The group stood before Knossos again, ready to begin their first assault—the very same passage in which that memory had occurred.

The air was tense. The hall was packed with adventurers, each ready to move at a moment's notice. They all awaited the signal to begin the assault.

Filvis stood among them, still struggling to unpack her feelings. She glanced at the girl standing to her side.

She was staring straight ahead, toward the gates of Knossos, hands wrapped tightly around her staff. Tense yet with a burning look of determination in her eyes.

"*Begin!*"

The voice of their commander issued from the crystal. The adventurers let out a chorus of cries. Filvis set off running with the girl at her side and swore an oath that no one could hear.

I will protect you.

With that vow in her heart, Filvis marched into the labyrinth where her fate awaited.

TO THE ONE I MET UPON A STORY'S PAGE

"So the six great spirits sang together and unleashed untold destruction? Is that what you're saying?"

"Y-yes...At least, that's what the story says..."

Tione's stern look elicited a confused nod from the white-haired boy. In the sunny streets of Orario, she and Tiona had just finished hearing an account of the "Spirits' Six-Ring" from Bell Cranell. That was the final piece of the puzzle they had been looking for.

Tione and Aiz nodded to each other. This was big. They said their farewells to Bell, then set off running, eager to inform Finn and the others as quickly as possible.

Only Tiona stayed behind, staring at Bell, as if he were the wise character from a hero story whose role was to help the main hero along with a piece of timely advice.

Then she clapped her hands around Bell's cheeks and squeezed.

"M-mish Tiona...?"

Bell wasn't quite sure what to make of the Amazonian girl massaging his cheeks. His face slowly turned red as Tiona studied his face, ignoring the nearby prum girl's cries of "Wh-what are you doing to Mr. Bell?!"

"How come you know everything, Argonaut?" she asked.

"Hwuh...?"

"I really gotta talk to you more often!"

Her sister called her name, and Tiona flashed a wide-eyed, beaming smile like that of a little child.

"Thank you!" she said. "We'll make sure your help is put to good use! Next time we meet, we can chat about stories again! We can laugh together again!"

And with one last smile and a wave, she departed, the resolve of a one-sided vow burning in her chest.

"What do you suppose all that was about?"

"…I don't know…"

After Tiona left, Lilly and Bell stood alone in a crowd of people.

"But I think," said Bell, "they're going on an adventure…At least, that's what it looked like to me…"

The stern look of the girl he admired and Tiona's sunny smile—both were etched into Bell's rubellite eyes. He could never forget them even if he tried.

If all was connected by fate, then the seeds of that fate had already been sown.

IN PLACE OF FLOWERS, THE WOLF HOWLS

The wind blew, rustling the flowers and delivering Bete's resolution to the dead who slept beneath.

He stood alone before a gravestone bathed in evening light, ready for battle in both body and mind. He wore his silver boots, Frosvirt, as well as the twin Unbreakables, Dual Roland.

All around him stretched the countless graves that made up the Adventurers Graveyard. The headstone at his feet read *Leene Arshe*.

Hers was surrounded by the graves of other fallen members of *Loki Familia*. Standing in their midst, Bete said nothing. He simply stood there in quiet contemplation.

"Good grief," came a voice from behind him. "There's no need for all this sneaking around, you know."

Bete turned to see Gareth, similarly dressed for battle but also holding a large bouquet of flowers. On the eve of their second great assault, he had come in Finn's place to offer the thoughts and prayers of *Loki Familia*'s top brass. Bete clicked his tongue, then turned and began walking away.

"You didn't see anything, old man," he growled. "Got that?"

"If that's how you want it, then very well," replied Gareth. "I won't tell a soul. However, I fear it may be a trifle too late."

Bete stopped in his tracks. The wolf ears atop his head twitched. He slowly turned and looked past Gareth's triumphant smile to the stooped-over hume bunny in his shadow, Rakuta.

"Awawawa!" she cried.

Bete said nothing. He strode over to her, grabbed her by the lapels, and lifted her off the ground.

"Speak a word of this, and I'll turn you into rabbit stew. Got it?"

"Erm...er...I..."

"Got it?!"

"Y-yes, sir!!"

Bete scowled and tossed Rakuta aside before stomping off for real this time.

"M-Mr. Bete!!"

Bete stopped again. There were tears in the hume bunny's eyes, though whether that was due to Bete's yelling or not was unclear.

"We will win this fight! I'm sure of it!" she shouted.

Bete turned and looked over his shoulder, a truly displeased scowl on his face, and yelled back, "Of course we will, dumbass!"

His roar carried across the sea of graves. Rakuta gave a teary-eyed smile, while Gareth's lips curled upward as well.

A HERO'S VOW

"Excuse me, Captain...Oh."

Finn heard a knock and sensed someone entering the room, but he didn't respond immediately. He was down on one knee, one hand placed across his breast like a knight swearing a solemn vow, kneeling before a tapestry on one wall and the stone bust that stood before it.

"I-I'm sorry, Captain. I didn't realize you were praying..."

"It's fine," said Finn, opening his eyes and standing up. "You're not the first to interrupt. I should have locked the door if I wanted to be undisturbed."

Finn cast a soft smile toward the doorway, where Tione was standing.

"Come to tell me everything is ready, I trust?"

"Yes, sir. All five units are ready to move out at any time."

Finn and Tione were both ready for battle, too, armed with their spear and Kukri knives, respectively.

It was the eve of war, the night before the second assault on Knossos. Outside the window, night cloaked the city. The blue light was at once an indigo sea and an azure flame.

"Were you...praying for victory from Lady Fianna?" asked Tione.

Fianna was a fictional goddess whom the prum worshipped. Finn's devotion to her was well-known among the familia, and he always prayed to her to bring glory to his race on the night before an important battle.

"No," Finn answered. "I was saying good-bye."

"...Pardon?"

Tione's eyes flew wide with surprise. They grew even wider after what Finn said next.

"I've stopped looking up to Fianna. Instead, I've sworn to become an even brighter beacon. I pray to ensure she watches over me in that endeavor."

Finn's smile looked prouder and more defiant than Tione had ever seen. In the blink of an eye, her cheeks flushed scarlet, and she smiled back.

"Do you find it offensive, Tione?"

"No! In fact, I think I fell in love with you all over again!"

"Then let's go. We're going to best a god today."

"Yes, sir!"

A love renewed and a hero reborn. The two set off for the front lines together.

EVE OF WAR

"Riveria. Leave that person to me."

It was on the eve of the second attack on Knossos that Aiz came to Riveria with that request.

They stood in the suspended corridor that ran between two of their manor's towers. Riveria had called Aiz here so that the two could speak one-on-one, beneath the sea of stars. Both had been assigned to unit two for the operation, but the high elf didn't answer Aiz immediately. She remained silent, her jade eyes displaying a look of worry for the girl's safety.

"…"

The person Aiz had referred to was their most fearsome foe, the creature Levis. If it had been up to Riveria, Aiz would never go anywhere near that dangerous woman, but there were six demi-spirits to contend with, and it simply wasn't possible to hold any forces in reserve. Moreover, it seemed the redheaded monster was targeting Aiz. The only option was to let her have her. Riveria was wise and had already considered all this.

"…As long as you don't die out there."

"I won't. I promise."

Aiz didn't break her gaze. She was like a sword, stubborn and unyielding. All Riveria could do was sigh.

"…Very well," she said. "Loki tells me your stats have come a long way in recent weeks."

"Riveria…Thank you."

Aiz breathed a soft sigh of relief.

"But I must ask," said Riveria. "How *did* you improve so much in such a short time? I hear your stats increased by over two hundred fifty apiece."

"Warlord taught me. I was practicing with him and..."

The elation of Riveria's acceptance caused Aiz to lower her guard for a moment, and by the time she realized what she'd let slip, it was too late. Riveria's soft smile vanished in an instant, replaced with a frigid gaze.

"I see," she said. "I did think it didn't match what you'd attained in the Dungeon...So that's how you did it."

Aiz had been training since before the first assault began, but she'd never told her fellow members about it, because she knew there was a 99 percent chance that Riveria would blow up at her if she did. It went without saying that any upstanding *Loki Familia* member cavorting with the backward barbarians at *Freya Familia* was committing a faux pas of the highest order.

Objection! Leading the witness! She set me up!

"R-Riveria, wait! I just wanted to improve!"

"How many times do I have to tell you? As a top member of this familia, you should think about how your actions will be perceived! It looks like I'm going to need to teach you another lesson, young lady."

Even before the battle had been joined, Aiz's screams could be heard echoing above the manor.

BEGINNER'S LUCK?

"What on earth are you lot up to?"

It was break time at The Benevolent Mistress, and Lyu passed a curious sight. Bell and Syr were seated at a round table, playing cards.

"Oh, hi, Ms. Lyu," said Bell, looking up from his hand with a strained smile. "The waitresses made me join in...I don't think I really get the rules, though..."

"Come on, white-hair! Avenge our deaths, meow!"

"Believe in the luck that carried you through the War Game and strike down this woman for her crimes, meow. Syr must die!"

"We're counting on you, adventurer boy!"

Her fellow waitresses, not counting Syr, gathered around Bell, cheering him on. Syr sat at the opposite end of the table, a triumphant smile spread across her lips.

"Remember, Bell. Whoever loses this hand has to do whatever the winner says. And wouldn't you know it? I have a full house right here!"

There wasn't a speck of mercy in her rabbit-hunting eyes. Cries of "Another good hand?! She's got the luck of the gods!" "It's over, it's all over, meow...!" and "Useless white-hair!" rang out from the other waitresses. Syr's uncanny ability to see through any lie or bluff had served her well in the game so far.

Bell looked at the cards in his hand and stammered. "Ah-ha-ha, I don't think I can win. I only have a pair..."

With a defeated smile, he revealed his hand face up on the table. They were the six of diamonds, followed by the seven, eight, and ten of the same suit, plus a joker. When Lyu saw the cards laid out, she was flabbergasted.

"M-Mr. Cranell! That's a straight flush!"

As soon as she said it, Bell and all the other waitresses went, """""Huh?"""""

It seemed that none of them quite grasped the rules. Had Lyu not been there, Bell's victory might have gone completely unnoticed. Little wonder, then, that Syr's ability was of no use; there was no point in detecting lies when even Bell didn't realize what his hand contained.

"You did it, white-hair!!"

"All right!!"

"Take that, Syr!!"

"Whaaaat?! How?!"

Ahnya, Chloe, and Runoa went wild, while Syr sat there with tears in her eyes. The unbelievable comeback resulted in Syr having to do the chores for all the other waitresses, while Lyu watched on in disbelief.

"No slacking! Get back to work, meow!"

"Why meee?!"

"Beginner's luck..." muttered Lyu. "What a terrifying thing..."

THE ILLUSIVE SECOND MASTER

"Thank you for agreeing to this training, Mr. Cranell."

"O-oh, no, please! The pleasure's all mine!"

It was early morning, before dawn's light had reached the tavern courtyard, when Bell and Lyu shook hands.

A few days after all the fuss at the casino had died down, Bell was making good on his promise. He had agreed to help Lyu with her training at the crack of dawn. At present, the elf was dressed plainly and armed with a wooden sword, while Bell held a blunted practice knife.

"I apologize for making you come out so early," said Lyu, "and for acquiescing to my selfish demands."

"N-not at all! I'm just glad I get to learn from a master like you!"

That wasn't flattery. If Bell ever hoped to catch up to the one he admired, then opportunities like this were exceedingly valuable.

Come to think of it, Aiz has been training me as well. I guess that makes Lyu my second master!

Bell was tickled pink by the notion, but the smile on his face was met by Lyu's serious expression.

"That's the spirit…If I'm to catch up to Syr…then I must hold nothing back, either."

"Huh?"

"I thought it would be useful for us to train alongside each other, but I've changed my mind. If we are both to improve, Mr. Cranell, we must practice sparring."

Bell failed to keep up with Lyu's sudden change of heart. By the time he noticed the unsettling mood that had descended over them, it was too late. The elf girl narrowed her eyes and spoke.

"...Here I come."

Bell didn't remember very much that came after that.

"Stand up. We go again."

"What are you lying there for? Again."

"The enemy will not stand still while you dawdle. Again."

"Again." "Again." "Again." "Again." "Again." "Again." "Again." "Again." "Again." "Again." "Again." "Again." "Again." "Again."

When Bell finally regained his senses, he was lying on the cold, hard ground, beaten black and blue.

Miss Lyu's training methods are pretty harsh as well...

There was no way a Level 3 boy could keep up with a Level 4 elf.

"...Perhaps I overdid it," muttered Lyu.

"'Overdid it'?" whispered Ahnya, watching on. "I think you purrty much killed him!"

Twenty seconds later, Syr walked in, saw Lyu silently standing over a battered Bell, and blew her top.

AND AT THAT MOMENT, LYU LEON SHIVERED

"Haah..."

Somewhere in the Labyrinth City, a single human girl gave a sultry sigh as she sat by the window of her house. The name of this lovely young lady was Anna Kreiz, and at this very moment, she was being watched by her parents standing in the hallway.

"Oh, what's got that girl so hot and bothered?" muttered the father, Huey. "She's been like that all day."

"Don't you recognize it, love?" replied the mother, Karen. "Men can be so insensitive sometimes." She smiled. "That's the face of a girl in love. I bet Anna's thinking of a lovely man she's met."

"A...a MAN?!"

Huey was so shocked, he sprang out of his chair, threw aside the newspaper he had been reading, and dashed into the room where Anna sat. All he could think of was the wonderful times they had spent together as father and daughter—and the horrid, wretched man who would take it all away.

Karen smiled and followed him into the room while Huey demanded an explanation.

"A-Anna?!" he asked in a mad voice. "Is it true? You've fallen in love?!"

"Father...Yes, it is."

Anna blushed deeply but nodded, causing her father to squeal like a little girl.

"And what's more," Anna went on, "I fear I have fallen in love with someone I shouldn't."

"Wh-what do you mean? Who is he?!"

Karen remained smiling. Huey looked like he was about to cry. Anna placed both hands on her reddening cheeks and spoke.

"Not he...*She*. The brave, dashing young woman who saved me."

Oh.

Oh.

As soon as they both realized it, Anna's parents froze, and their faces grew grim. This was the fabled yuri of which the gods spoke!

At long last, Huey got over his initial shock enough to speak.

"...Well, at least it's not some man..."

"Excuse me, dear?!"

Karen suddenly got a ferocious look on her face. While the two parents started bickering, Anna turned back to the window and heaved another heavy sigh, laden with love.

THE NIGHT BEFORE A GRAND CASINO INFILTRATION

"Thank you so much, Mr. Allen!"

How many times had Allen wanted to punch this gray-haired girl right in her smiling face? But through colossal effort, he stayed his hand, causing his shoulders to quiver.

"I can't believe you came all this way just to bring me an invitation to the casino!"

"You were the one who threatened me to get a hold of it in the first place," Allen spat back.

"'Threatened'? Of course not! All I did was hint that it would be great if someone did it for me."

"Coming from you, it's all the same."

Syr's mercurial nature caused Allen to heave an uncharacteristic sigh. It was evening, and the two were standing in a shadowy alley at the tavern's rear entrance. Allen had taken great pains to procure an entry ticket at Syr's "request." It went without saying that the girl intended to poke her nose into places it shouldn't be.

And since Allen was supposed to protect Syr, that meant more work for him, too. As much as he wanted to talk her out of it, there was a reason he couldn't.

The Grand Casino? I've heard stories about that place that'll make your stomach turn. Now Hedin wants me to sneak in and investigate the owner? And since I owe him, I can't say no. What a pain in the ass...

For all his grievances, Allen really did care about the young girl's safety. And in the end, he *did* infiltrate the casino, unbeknownst to the young boy and the elf girl who were there at the same time. Ultimately, though, his shadowy vigil was wasted, as the elf and the rabbit rounded up the owner and his conspirators without Allen's help.

It was unclear whether Syr realized Allen's annoyance as she shifted to an altogether different smile.

"Would you like to come in?" she asked. "Ahnya's on the clock today, you know?"

"…"

A terrifying scowl filled with hate appeared on Allen's face, but the girl didn't even flinch. Then Allen sighed at her proposed family reunion.

"I've done what you asked for," he said. "I'm leaving."

"Very well. Thank you again, Mr. Allen."

Only Allen could detect the sincere gratitude and concern for his well-being lurking in those words, and it made his lips curl into a grudging smile.

QUADRUPLET THEATER

"We four brothers are in desperate need of some character differentiation."

""""What's this about, Alfrik?""""

"We're some of the mightiest prums in all the realm, and yet we're never spoken of except in the same breath."

"I've certainly heard of one sore loser who claimed we were cowardly curs for ganging up on him."

"Well, we'll teach him a lesson later."

"We've said time and time again we are one soul in four bodies, yet the ignorant masses don't understand."

"But it's true. We all look and sound the same. People say they can't even tell us apart and that we might as well not have first names and just go by The Gullivers."

""""What?!""""

"That's why I say we're in dire need of differentiation. Even I don't want my achievements to be lumped in with those of my foolish siblings."

"We'll deal with you later, Alfrik."

"But he has a point."

"All right, then let's distinguish ourselves! Let me hear you roar!!"

"I admire the part of you that latches on so quickly to any half-formed idea that comes your way, Grer."

"But even if we're talking about differentiation, how are we supposed to do it? It's a lazy idea, but what if we all talk in drastically different ways?"

"That would do the trick. But if we're all going to adopt some clever catchphrase, then we should agree on a theme, right?"

"A theme..."

"What is Lady Freya most into these days...Rabbits, maybe?"

""""That's it!"""""

"Why don't we all *hop* down to the Dungeon?"

"Berling, you *hare*brain! That's what I was going to pick!"

"You're no better, Dvalinn! You're *ear*-redeemable!"

"That's a real groaner, Grer! Um, let's see...I bet you thought you were *hare*-larious!"

""""Bad Alfrik!!!"""""

"What? Why?!"

"That's the same as Dvalinn's!"

"You can't just steal my idea!"

"Have you no shame?"

"You all just hate me because I'm the oldest! I've had enough—wait, is that Lady Freya?!"

"All right, let's show Lady Freya the new and improved Gulliver Brothers!"

"Why, you're looking delightful as always, Lady Freya! Enough to make a man *hopping* mad!"

"Absolutely stunning, Milady! Did you do something to your...*hare*?"

"You look *ear*-resistable!"

"Erm...*Hare*-lo, Lady Freya!"

"Why on earth are you all putting so much effort into sounding completely insufferable today? And I still can't tell the four of you apart."

""""N-nooooo!"""""

WAR STORIES FROM SINDH: NOTES LEFT BY A TERRORIZED WARSA SOLDIER

On the sandy plains of Sindh, the Third Division was stationed along the right-hand flank of the Warsa army. It was there the troops bore witness to a terrible nightmare.

"Gwaaaaaaaaaghhh!!"

Their forces were being slaughtered by a single dark elf—*Freya Familia*'s first-tier adventurer, Hegni Ragnar.

Ordinarily, this elf was anxious, awkward, and neurotic, but when he activated his spell, *Dáinsleif*, Hegni transformed into an undisputed lord of the battlefield.

With a single lunge, he scattered dust into the air, and with one swing of his blade, he tore through the enemy ranks. The mere sight of him was so terrifying that even though the battle had only just begun, the morale of the Warsa army was plummeting.

Soldiers and mercenaries who had started the skirmish crying, "Wretched outsider! We shall show you the strength of the desert!" were now screaming and fleeing for their lives, desperate not to be caught in the calculated sights of their foe.

Amid all the chaos, Hegni thought to himself.

Even without the darkness, I am the darkness. This battle unfolds according to my every whim. Not a single soul shall know peace. Next, to the east...

Although his thought process was a little different while he was under the effect of his spell, Hegni was still the same person at his core. It was only for convenience that he used the name Dáinsleif to refer to his alter ego; in truth, the man's superior tactical and strategic acumen aligned with Hegni's own.

I shall offer their heads on plates, thus proving my loyalty to my lady. Then I shall be allowed to rest my head on her soft thighs. Thighs, thighs, thighs...

Unfortunately, this sometimes resulted in the wires getting a little crossed and Hegni's and Dáinsleif's thoughts becoming mixed.

"Give me your thighs. Let me offer up your thighs. My goddess's thighs are not yours; they are mine."

"AAAAAAAAAAWHATTHEHELLISHESAYINGAAAA-AAAA!!!"

"Gah...shit! I took an arrow to the thigh!"

"Is that so? Then die."

"Gaaaaaaaaaaagh!!"

In the end, most of the Third Division fell to lethal thigh wounds, and one record of the battle caused future archaeologists to scratch their heads.

It read, *The nightmare of the desert came for our thighs.*

AFTER THE DESERT JOURNEY: ELVEN DEBRIEFING

Royman Mardeel, head of the Guild, had a stomachache.

He wanted to swallow some medicine right now.

For standing in his office on the very top floor of Guild HQ was one man: *Freya Familia*'s first-tier adventurer and fellow elf, Hedin Selland.

"Our Lady Freya has been brought back to Orario, safe and sound. We didn't suffer any losses, either. What are you so annoyed about?"

"For breaking the rules, leaving the city without a word…Lord Ouranos will not be pleased, you know!"

"If he finds out, then all your dirty little secrets Freya was able to blackmail you with will be aired out like filthy laundry, pig."

"Grh…!"

When Freya first left for the Kaios Desert, she had made a deal with Royman. Then when her first-tier adventurers wanted to know where she went, it was Hedin who had burst into Royman's office, demanding an explanation. *"Why did you let Lady Freya out of the city? If she didn't charm you, then she must know some secrets you can't stand to be leaked. What are they? Tell me them now,"* he said, calmly yet driven to madness by worry, *"or I'll kill you."*

It was only due to Hedin's ingenuity (and Royman's indiscretion) that the leaders of *Freya Familia* were able to pick up on their goddess's trail so quickly.

Out of all the elves, few were more terrified of Hedin than Royman was. The man seemed oddly quick to anger, and any random thing could set him off. When the terrifying man ripped off Royman's spectacles and crushed them, it was already over. Yet it also seemed like there was a part of Hedin's mind that recognized and utilized his own anger from a place of rational detachment. If it was up to Royman, he would take that high-elf runaway princess over Hedin any day of the week. Out of all *Freya Familia*'s wild beasts, Hedin was the one Royman hated dealing with the most. How many times had he been driven to exhaustion by the elf's outrageous demands?

"Come to think of it, I had to deal with someone very much like you on my trip," said Hedin, "albeit even more loathsome, if you can imagine such a thing. Do you want me to try the same methods that worked so well on him?"

"Th-that won't be necessary! This is the most terrifying traveler's tale I've ever heard! What did you do to this man anyway?"

"I let the others temper him until he became a second Ottar, only smaller and weaker."

"The scariest thing is that I actually understand what you mean by that incomprehensible gibberish!! Your 'training' should be classified as cruel and unusual punishment! What else did you get up to on this misadventure of yours?!"

"We exterminated an army of eighty thousand with only eight. There were people watching, too."

Royman began frothing at the mouth, his eyes rolling back in his head as he collapsed onto the floor.

And Royman's regular order of stomach medicine increased in size yet again after that day.

IT'S TOUGH BEING THE CAPTAIN

"She's freed all the slaves in the market..." muttered Alfrik, standing beside Ottar.

An incredible cheer arose from the marketplace before them. Having followed the trail of their goddess into the Kaios Desert, the top-tier adventurers of *Freya Familia* now stood atop a rooftop in the town of Leodo, watching the aftermath of Freya's stunning declaration. She had just bought every last slave in the city, and the grateful people were crying and shouting in joy.

Each of Freya's children was left speechless, except for Hedin. "From reading her lips, it appears she wishes to buy the mansion as well," he said, adjusting his spectacles. This caused the others to fall even more silent.

"...Hedin, can we even afford that?" asked Ottar.

"We can. Barely. We will have to cut back in several places, though."

"Heh-heh-heh...We cannot have Lady Freya's tributes wearing thin," said Hegni.

"Quite. But shut up."

"When we get back to Orario, we ought to head into the Dungeon some more and pick up some extra cash...But I just ordered a new set of equipment..."

"Me too."

"Me three."

"Me four."

Ottar turned and looked to the rest of his juniors.

"I have a mission when we get back," said Allen dismissively.

"Heh-heh-heh…I'm afraid fate has already spelled out a path for my blade…"

"Hegni and I have already agreed on terms for a couple of forays into the depths," said Hedin. "We did it on goodwill, so don't expect much in the way of cash."

Ottar curled his lip.

"Just put the juniors to work," said Allen. "If you say jump, they'll fall over each other to ask how high."

"Although by then, they'll all be in the Dungeon…"

"…And who knows what kind of trouble they'll get into…"

"…Plus, they could run into *Loki Familia* like last time…"

"…And not to mention the amount of work that'll cause for Hörn and Heith."

"Heh-heh-heh…The curse of a priestess and a witch's bolt of lightning…Both will fall upon your head, Ottar."

"Quite. Though I'm sure that's not too much for you to handle."

""""""""We'll leave it to you, boar man.""""""""

Had Ottar snapped right then and there, it would have been completely understandable.

MISCELLANEOUS

FIVE YEARS AFTER: AIZ WALLENSTEIN
5th Anniversary Special Story Collection: On the Side

PATHS SO FAR, AN UNENDING JOURNEY
Kiyotaka Haimura Illustrations: The Art of Sword Oratoria

MIRAGE IN A SEA OF SAND
DanMachi Collection Extra 2021 (Square Enix Manga Campaign)

FIVE YEARS AFTER: AIZ WALLENSTEIN

It was a dream.
Aiz could tell immediately.
She was a little older now, on the road with Riveria. Somewhere other than Orario. They traveled over rolling hills, through stunning vistas, and toward windmilled villages on the horizon. The sky overhead was peaceful, blue, and mild.
Aiz and Riveria smiled at each other like mother and child.
A happy dream.

It was a dream.
Aiz could tell immediately.
A slightly more mature Aiz sat outside a café, chatting with Tiona, Tione, and Lefiya. Tiona was laughing like she always did. Tione was still chasing after the man of her dreams. And Lefiya was sipping tea gracefully from a ceramic cup.
Aiz was happy, watching them all, wearing a smile more mellow than ever before.
A gentle dream.

It was a dream.
Aiz could tell immediately.
She lay, bleeding, in the depths of the Dungeon, still and unmoving. As did her friends Finn, Riveria, Gareth, Tiona, Tione, Bete, and Lefiya—her entire familia.

The evils of the Dungeon had claimed them all, draining their life and annihilating them.

Aiz shut her eyes, knowing it would be the last time.

A harrowing dream.

It was a dream.

Aiz could tell immediately. It was too strange to be real.

Aiz was an adult and had become a queen.

She ruled deep in a secluded forest, over a fairy village built into a holy spring. There she sat atop her throne, stone-faced, like a doll, as identityless fairies flew through the air or played in the spring waters, cheering her reign. Draped only in white cloth, with a crown of ivy atop her head.

She said, "Whee," raising her staff and emitting a strange light as she frolicked with the joyous sprites.

Aiz nearly spluttered herself awake.

An incomprehensible dream.

Was this a dream?

At first, Aiz couldn't tell.

There were swords, spears, axes, staffs, and shields stuck into the wasteland like grave markers. Aiz was surrounded by them.

One of her arms had been torn off. One of her eyes had been plucked out. She was full of holes and covered in blood. Surrounded by half-disintegrated weapons, she faced the darkness alone.

With fierce determination in her one good eye, Aiz raised her sword high. She spat blood and screamed her heart's greatest wish as the storm winds rose, and her silver sword shone.

But, like blowing out a candle, a wave of darkness stole her away—and that was it. The dream fell apart.

To Aiz, that terrible dream was far more compelling than any other. As if she knew that was the one that awaited her…The fate she could never avoid.

* * *

Eventually, once all the other dreams receded, Aiz had another dream.

It was a person.

As she kneeled, Aiz looked up to see a person standing before her, their back turned.

She didn't know why, but she knew who they were.

It was a hero who fought for her sake.

Softly, quietly, Aiz awoke. A shaft of light peeked through white curtains. Outside, she heard the songs of little birds. It was morning.

Aiz didn't remember her dreams in detail, but she recalled feeling happy, sad, and confused.

What was waiting for her five years down the line? Ten? Twenty?

Aiz got up, grabbed her sword, unsheathed it, and stood like a knight, eyes closed.

Then the swordswoman opened the door, ready to take one more step toward her future, whatever it may be.

PATHS SO FAR, AN UNENDING JOURNEY

One day, Aiz was walking through the city without a particular destination in mind. It was such a beautiful day that it seemed a shame to waste it, so she left early to make the most of the time before her Dungeon foray.

She strolled through the Main Streets, crossed Central Park, and went down side streets and back alleys until she arrived on the east side of the city, a place she didn't often visit.

Aiz had great fun spotting all these streets she'd never noticed before, when at last, her wandering led her to a familiar location.

"I'm here..."

It was during the Monsterphilia, over two months earlier. Aiz had fought a horde of carnivorous plants at this exact spot. She had gotten into trouble, and it was Lefiya who'd saved her.

There was no trace, now, of the damage that battle had left. The city had paved over the cracked stones, and the holes in the sides of the buildings had been completely repaired. The street was alive with the sounds of people once more.

But just then, two Guild employees walked up to her.

"Is that Ms. Wallenstein?"

"Oh, yes, it is! Hello there!"

"Miss Eina...and Ms. Misha?"

One was the half-elf Eina Tulle, and the other was her colleague, the human Misha Frot. Aiz recognized them both, the former due to some personal business and the latter as a Guild receptionist who interacted with her familia on official business.

Both women were in uniform and greeted Aiz with smiles.

"Are you heading out today?" asked Eina.

"Yes," Aiz replied. "What about you two…?"

"We've been sent to inspect this whole area," said Eina. "In particular, this street, which suffered heavy damage during the Monsterphilia."

"Some of the monsters got out and caused chaos!" added Misha. "It could have been really bad!" Then, after looking Aiz over, Misha remembered something. "Oh yeah! You were there, Ms. Wallenstein! You were so cool! You beat 'em all up like *bam-bam-bam*!"

"Your professionalism could use some work, Misha," Eina cautioned. "But you're right. You really helped us out back then, Ms. Wallenstein. Allow me to extend my thanks on behalf of the Guild."

Eina smiled, creasing the emerald eyes behind her spectacles. Misha bowed and said, "Thank you very much!" leaving Aiz unsure how to respond. As far as she was concerned, she had only done what was expected of any able-bodied adventurer living in Orario. That and she wasn't used to being thanked so directly. Just as Aiz's muddled thoughts were beginning to show on her unexpressive face, all of a sudden, a young animal girl ran up to her out of the crowd.

"Nice lady!"

"…?"

At first, Aiz was confused, but then she recognized the girl.

She was with her mother now, but when Aiz first met her, she had been in serious danger of being eaten by a carnivorous plant.

"Thank you so much for saving me!" the girl said. "I thought I'd never get to thank you!"

It was obvious from her smile and gestures that she had been waiting for a long time to tell Aiz how grateful she was. Her mother stood nearby, echoing the girl's sincere thanks.

"You and the other nice ladies were so pretty and strong! I want to be just like you when I grow up! A brave hero who saves people!"

Eina and Misha watched on, silently admiring the heartwarming scene. Aiz looked shocked for a moment, before taking the little girl's thanks to heart.

"Thank you for keeping everyone safe, nice lady!"

"...You're welcome."

Aiz gave a gentle smile, and the little girl blushed and beamed back.

Leaving the warmth of the surface behind, Aiz descended into the Dungeon to hone her skills in live combat. The upper levels posed little challenge to her, and very soon, she was on floor eighteen, otherwise known as Under Resort, the crystal-filled caverns located roughly halfway through the middle levels.

This naturally occurring safety point was filled with trees and forests. Aiz let her eyes wander, and when she spotted the large tree growing in the center of the floor, she decided this would make a good place for a short rest. With that in mind, she headed to the checkpoint town of Rivira. As soon as she set foot on its roads of stone and crystal, however, she ran into the town's leader, Bors Elder.

"Hey there, Sword Princess! Haven't seen you down here in a while! How go things?"

"Bors..."

Bors was a giant of a man with a seemingly permanent scowl, but he was amicable enough once you got to know him. He gestured at the town behind him.

"What do you think? Pretty good, right? You can hardly tell you punks came through here with all those monsters and caused all that damage! Don't hesitate to use this place again!"

Rivira had been all but destroyed in an attack conducted by one creature woman and a bunch of carnivorous plants. Now, however, it was as good as new—perhaps even better than new, given how many more high-level adventurers were frequenting the place than ever before.

That was because *Loki Familia* had managed to reach parts of the Dungeon that had been untouched since Zeus and Hera's time, and it seemed that this success had breathed new life into the adventurers and their ambitions. It was none other than adventurers, after all, who made Rivira the sordid yet beautiful place it was.

All of a sudden, however, Aiz recalled something.

"What happened to Udaeus's sword...?" she asked.

Udaeus was a Monster Rex of the deep levels. A monster that Aiz had defeated single-handedly. After obtaining its sword, Aiz had entrusted the rare drop to Bors, something of a weapon enthusiast in these parts. Bors had promised he could make a killer weapon out of the remains, but as soon as Aiz asked about it, great beads of sweat appeared on his face.

"O-o-o-oh, that?! I just...er...It needs a little more time in the oven, or should I say...you can't just expect me to hammer something out overnight...or maybe you should stop putting so much pressure on me...! A-a-a-anyway, the point is it's not done yet!"

Bors gave the biggest fake smile he could, then turned and ran away. If Aiz didn't know any better, it almost seemed like he was trying to hide something.

"..."

Aiz silently tilted her head. Then she took a look around.

"This is where I first met her..."

Levis—the red-haired creature who knew the truth behind Aiz's origin. It was right here in Rivira that Aiz had encountered her for the first time. The woman was after Aiz, and every time she struck, bodies were left in her wake. Feeling her fists tighten, Aiz looked toward the north end of the town, toward Cluster Street, where she and Levis had crossed swords for the very first time. It was one of Rivira's most prominent locations, a place where the crystals formed a natural valley. After a few seconds, Aiz turned and started walking.

She couldn't explain why, but before she knew it, Aiz was standing before a tavern on the outskirts of town. The sign out front depicted a cave mouth, along with the establishment's name: The Golden Cellar.

Aiz opened the door and stepped inside, only to run into a chienthrope girl with tanned skin.

"Oh, Sword Princess? It *is* you!"

"Ms. Lulune…And Ms. Asfi's here as well?"

"Hey. What a coincidence, meeting you here."

It was Lulune Louie, and the bespectacled human girl was Asfi Al Andromeda. They were not alone, either, and several other adventurers were present, whom Aiz quickly realized were other members of *Hermes Familia*. All were gathered around a particularly large table, drinking and chatting merrily.

Aiz spotted Falgar the weretiger, Merrill the prum, Nelly the human, among others. They all welcomed Aiz warmly, and Asfi flashed the girl a smile as well.

"What are you all doing here?" Aiz asked.

"Mmm…We just happened to have some free time, that's all. We figured we'd come down here and share a drink. Pour one out for those who can't be with us anymore, that sort of thing…"

"…"

Aiz could never forget the tragedy that occurred in the pantry on the twenty-fourth floor. Aiz, along with *Hermes Familia*, had taken on a quest to respond to a mass outbreak of Irregulars. There, they had encountered Levis as well as the second creature, Olivas Act. Many of *Hermes Familia*'s brave adventurers lost their lives in the mortal struggle that followed.

This bar had been where Aiz met up with the group—the very last place where those unfortunate members had enjoyed a drink. It was no surprise, then, that their surviving comrades would come here to remember them.

Aiz remembered the faces of those she had fought alongside, and a bitter look crossed her features.

"Don't cry, Sword Princess," said Lulune, waving her hand with a smile. "We didn't come here to weep."

"We have to keep moving on," said Asfi. "We don't have time to cry over the past. We have to laugh." She chuckled. "And raise our cups to the heavens and say, 'What fools you are to be missing this!'"

Aiz couldn't believe what she was hearing. Lulune was one thing, but she'd never heard Perseus crack a joke in all her days. Then she realized. It wasn't just a joke. This was their way of mourning, of overcoming the sorrow caused by their old friends' absence. It was an adventurer's way: lacking tact yet undeniably heartfelt.

"We'd be grateful if you keep them in your thoughts, too, Sword Princess," said Asfi. "That'll be our way of honoring their memories."

"Because we adventurers have got to stick together," said Lulune.

"Go on ahead," said Falgar.

"Visit all the places they never got to go," said Nelly.

"And then," said Merrill, "tell them what you saw."

Each of them wore tender smiles that hid painful memories. Aiz nodded.

"I will…"

After leaving Rivira and spending several hours wandering with no goal in mind, admiring the scenery of Under Resort, Aiz decided to wrap up her business in the Dungeon and return to the surface.

Despite the many thoughts weighing on her mind, she ascended the Dungeon's floors without much effort, until she reached the ninth floor in the upper levels. There, while walking the beaten path between floors, she suddenly stopped. Up ahead, she could hear sounds. Not the cries of monsters but people's voices.

Confused, Aiz began to approach, when suddenly, she received a big surprise.

"C'mon, big guy, you *sure* you don't need a weapon forged?"

"…"

"Guys like you must need a new sword made every week. Bet they don't last, do they?"

"..."

"So c'mon, let our forges help you out."

It was the cyclopean smith, Tsubaki...and Ottar of *Freya Familia*. The two were standing side by side, having a conversation—or half of one, anyway. It was such a bizarre sight that it stopped Aiz in her tracks. These were two people she had never expected to see together. Granted, the smiths at *Hephaistos Familia* would accept a job from anybody if it piqued their interest, but seeing the stone-faced boaz next to the carefree half-dwarf made for such a surreal composition that Aiz couldn't believe her eyes at first. She stood there, stunned, until Tsubaki noticed her.

"Hm? Oh, if it isn't Sword Princess!"

To be completely honest, Aiz had hoped she could slip by unseen, but it wasn't to be. Once Tsubaki called out to her, Ottar silently came over. That broke Aiz out of her stupor, and she squared off for battle.

"Sword Princess..."

The two-meder giant towered over Aiz, his rust-colored eyes boring into her. His overwhelming presence reminded Aiz of the time they had crossed swords—of the time they had done battle, right here on this very floor.

Aiz waited with bated breath for Ottar's next words. They turned out to be a question.

"I heard Udaeus left you a sword," he muttered. "...Is that true?"

Aiz could only blink several times in surprise. At length, she awkwardly nodded.

"There must be some reason for that," Ottar said. "Can you think of one?"

"...Maybe...because I fought it alone...?"

"I see. You have my thanks."

And with that, Ottar brushed her shoulder and walked away. This man was the greatest adventurer in the city, a man who had once tried to kill Aiz for the mere offense of affiliating with *Loki Familia*. Now he left in peace, disappearing deeper into the Dungeon without even a supporter by his side.

"Stiff as a board, that man," Tsubaki lamented. "He's never shown a shred of courtesy in all the time I've known him. He didn't even answer any of my questions."

Aiz returned her gaze to the eyepatched smith, who almost seemed to be sulking. She quickly recovered and offered Aiz a cheery smile. "Good day to you, by the way. Didn't mean to ignore you like that."

Aiz nodded. "Ms. Tsubaki," she said. "You and him…"

"We just happened to meet on this floor," replied Tsubaki. "I figured I'd shoot my shot, but you saw how that ended. I don't think he's come down here in a while. Maybe *someone's* great exploits have spurred him to action once more?"

Tsubaki grinned, and Aiz went silent. "And you, Ms. Tsubaki…?" she asked.

"Just breaking in one of my latest creations," Tsubaki replied, waving a long *naginata* in one hand and a bulging sack in the other. "And gathering some new materials while I'm down here."

Aiz was characteristically curt with her questioning, but Tsubaki was so used to it by now she could almost read her thoughts. After explaining her business, Tsubaki grinned and set off down the Dungeon trail.

"I'd better get going," she said. "Next time you folks go on an expedition, take me along, yeah?"

After watching her disappear, Aiz turned and resumed walking.

She retraced the same path that had brought her home after her groundbreaking expedition. Memories of her meeting with Warlord stirred in her mind, and as if the memories were guiding her, she arrived before long at a familiar room.

It was the very site where a raging bull had been put to rest. The place where an adventurer had been born.

"Ah..."

When she arrived, a single adventurer boy stood there.

"...Bell."

"...Ms. Aiz?"

The white-haired boy looked up, a look of surprise on his face. There was no sign of his fellow party. Had he come down here alone? As Aiz walked over, he turned to face her.

"Is no one with you?" Aiz asked.

"N-no," replied Bell. "It was supposed to be a day off today, but...I just got the itch to come down here..."

Bell was now a second-tier adventurer. If he wanted, he could probably make it all the way down to the middle levels on his own. He was no longer the weak young boy who had once fought a minotaur in this exact spot. Thinking of how much he'd grown, Aiz smiled.

Meanwhile, Bell was looking around the room. "I don't know why I came back here..." he muttered. "I just felt like...I had to."

The boy let the room's stale air wash over him. As if he were standing where it all began. At the point where many diverging paths originated. Aiz cast her mind back, as well, to the face of the boy who had once refused her hand and stood up by himself. To the man who reminded her so much of her father—of a hero.

The excitement...and the loneliness both came rushing back.

"Thank you," she said.

"Huh?"

"You saved us."

"...I did?"

Bell looked baffled. It was something he didn't know. Something he didn't need to know. How his brave deeds had inspired the rest of *Loki Familia* to stand up and fight. How his actions had lit a fire in their hearts and allowed them to strike down the corrupted spirits.

The only thing Aiz could do at that moment was offer her deepest thanks to the boy who had grown so much in such a short time and would continue to do so.

After a short while, Bell recovered his composure. His face transformed from that of a bashful young boy into that of a brave adventurer who kept running, no matter what stood in his way.

"Erm…Ms. Aiz," he asked. "Are you…returning to the surface?"

"Yeah, I am."

"Then…I suppose I'll see you up top. I'm heading on."

The adventurer, a babe only recently born, smiled. Aiz smiled back and offered him some encouraging words.

"See you later…" she replied. "…And good luck."

The afternoon had worn on by the time Aiz reached the surface, and soon, the orange light of evening began to creep across the sky. Aiz exited Babel into Central Park, but when she did, she heard a commotion coming from the southwest.

"…Hm?"

Curious, Aiz wandered over to see what the fuss was about. The southwestern districts were known for how much business they saw, whether it was everyday necessities or rare luxuries that changed hands. As Aiz passed through the marketplace, however, she became aware of a tumult quite unlike the usual peddler's fare.

It was the sound of adventurers running through the streets barking orders at each other. Aiz quickly spotted their emblems and recognized them as followers of Ganesha, the elephant god.

Just as she was wondering what had them in such a hurry, a merchant suddenly called out to her.

"You there, beautiful adventurer! Could a freshly caught dodobass satisfy your needs? To tell you the truth, I caught this beautiful specimen just this morn with my very own pole!!"

"Hm…?"

"Feast your eyes on its glorious scales! Its tasteful size! This fish has surely come as a gift from the gods ab—*Erk*!"

Suddenly, the peddler—a human man—cut his spiel short. A glimmer of recognition crossed his eyes as he stared at Aiz. His spectacles slipped from his nose, his oval face paled in an instant, and great torrents of sweat began dripping down his face.

"'Ere, Rubart, how many times 'ave I told ye to leave the sales pitches to—Hey, wait. Well, if it en't the Sword Princess!"

"It's you…Mr. Rod."

The man who appeared was a veritable giant, looking as though he spent all his time out at sea, and Aiz recognized him immediately. This man was from Port Meren, and he was the captain of *Njörðr Familia*. He had assisted Aiz on a previous occasion, when, seeking information about the mass spawn of carnivorous plants, the girl left the city to investigate the regions around Lake Lolog.

"Never thought we'd meet again in a place like this!" said Rod. "Do you adventurer types often come around these parts?"

"Not usually…" Aiz replied. "And…who's this?"

"Hm? Oh, that's Rubart. Used to head up the Guild branch over in Meren."

"R-Rod! Don't go blabbing about that!"

"Oh."

Aiz remembered him. His full name was Rubart Ryan, and he had helped *Njörðr Familia* with the carnivorous plant outbreak. He once enjoyed a cushy job but was summarily dismissed when it was discovered that he'd been embezzling and smuggling magic stones.

Aiz remembered hearing from Loki that Njörðr had put him to work to atone for his misdeeds…So this was what that meant.

The man was a bureaucrat through and through. Riveria had once described him as "more high-strung than an elven lyre." Now, however, the man had earned a faint tan, and his wiry limbs were beginning to show some muscle. He'd even traded in his stuffed suit for a pair of fisherman's slacks, a plain tunic, and a headband.

"When he first showed up, he was moanin' up a storm," said Rod. "But you shoulda seen him his first day with a rod in his hands.

Bleedin' natural, he was. You saw how in his element he was a second ago, didn't ye?"

"Wow..."

"Don't look at me like that!" Rubart wailed. "I'll not have your pity! Aaagh!"

Aiz had meant it as genuine admiration, but Rod didn't take it that way, and he immediately began rolling on the floor in agony. Rod explained that these "attacks" came whenever Rubart was forced to remember his old job. Perhaps he was struggling to reconcile the awakening of his new talents with the pride he placed in his previous position.

However, Aiz was struck with something else: the speed with which the disgraced bureaucrat had settled into his new role.

It hasn't even been that long since the incident in Meren, she thought. But just as her mind drifted to the subject of people and how quickly they could change...

"What's this? Is Rubart having one of his panic attacks again? Oh, well here's a new face."

"Lord Njörðr..."

With little concern for Rubart's plight, the fair-faced deity strolled up as though he'd just returned from a business negotiation.

"With the rest of the familia..." noted Aiz.

"Yep. We've all come to sell our catches," said Njörðr. "Never expected to run into you here, though."

In the blink of an eye, the god turned grave.

"I must apologize, you know, for getting all you involved in that accursed mess."

"It's fine..."

"The boys and I have been talking, like, trying to come up with a new way of fishing. A way that doesn't mean we have to fight fire with fire." Njörðr scratched his head and smiled. "So just you wait and see. We'll cook up something special."

Faced with the god's blinding goodness, Aiz smiled back. She had a feeling things were going to be much busier in Meren from now on.

Just then, she finally remembered what had been gnawing at her mind for a while.

"Erm...Do you know why there are so many adventurers around today?" she asked.

"Oh, that..." said Njörðr, somewhat evasive. He sounded reluctant to speak more. Not out of shame, exactly, but as if he thought it was something Aiz was better off not knowing. "...Take it from me," he said at last. "I don't think you should hang around if you can help it."

"*I* shouldn't...?"

"Well, I mean anyone from your crew, really. I don't think they'd start a fight, but...things might get dicey."

Njörðr's words left more questions than answers. "Well, I've said my piece," he declared, then he and the other fishermen departed, dragging their carts and the still-raving Rubart behind them.

Aiz was curious what he meant, but she took Njörðr's warning to heart and left the marketplace as well. Shortly after, she heard someone calling out her alias in strangely accented Koine.

"Sword Princess!"

Aiz turned to see a fierce-looking Amazon, hurtling her way.

"Halt...Sword Princess! Or else...you die!"

"?!"

Aiz was shaken. At the same time, she recognized who it was.

Oh...it's her.

Long hair, the color of sand. Strikingly revealing clothing. A pair of eyes that were slitted like a snake's. This woman had deep ties to Tiona and Tione, a proud warrior from the isle of Telskyura—and her name was Argana Kalif.

"Finn!"

"Wha...?"

"Where is Finn?"

"'Finn'?"

"The prum who defeated me! The most striking, mighty, and adorable male in all the lands! Tell me where he is!"

Argana came closer and closer, pressing Aiz to respond. Her eyes were wild, her cheeks flushed, and she licked her lips like a serpent, all bewildering Aiz even more.

Was it just her imagination, or was this woman nothing like she was before?!

"Tell me! Now!"

"P-probably...over..."

Aiz weakly raised a finger in the direction of the Twilight Manor. Argana exclaimed, "Over there?!" and immediately put her Level 6 athleticism to good use, barreling off toward the north of the city.

Aiz blankly watched her go, then all of a sudden, there was a second voice.

"Sword Princess!"

Again?!

This time, Aiz noticed Argana's twin sister, Bache, running down the street toward her. She realized this because the Amazon nearly crashed into her and sent her flying.

"Nal raz Argana! Dono gofa?!"

Oh, she's asking about her sister...

Aiz couldn't make heads or tails of the barrage of Amazonian words that came her way, but she managed to pick out Argana's name and piece together the rest. She raised her finger once more in the same direction as she had only a few seconds earlier.

Bache said, "Seh roo!"—words of thanks, hopefully—and ran off with blinding speed. Shattering the flagstones, she leaped onto the rooftops and continued her pursuit. Before long, Aiz heard the raised voices of the city watch:

"Did anyone see the Amazons who forced their way into the city?"

"We've rounded up everyone except those two twins!"

"How did they manage to break through the front gates?!"

"That's the fifth time this week!"

"Letting them run loose is a blot upon our name!"

"I am Ganesha!"

And so on. Aiz started sweating bullets as it slowly dawned on her what, exactly, all the prior fuss had been about.

"Those twins will be the death of me," came a weary voice. "They've become a couple of wild beasts in heat..."

A young girl appeared before Aiz, with dark brown skin and black hair. She wore a pale blue one-piece dress and directed a wicked glare at Aiz.

"...and it's all your fault, *Loki Familia*!"

The girl looked sweet and innocent enough, but the moment she opened her mouth, it became clear she was beyond precocious. Aiz stared at her in shock, having never seen the girl before, until the child made a disgruntled "mrgh" and took something out of her pocket.

"Recognize me now?"

"Oh...Lady Kali?"

The moment she put on the fang-covered mask, Aiz's eyes went wide. The little girl had none of the gravitas of other gods and could probably blend into a crowd of mortals with little effort. Argana and Bache's god seemed pleased to be finally recognized, though, and gave a satisfied nod of approval.

"This hair is a wig, by the way," she said. "It's all part of my cunning disguise."

"...Okay? Why are you here?"

"To follow Argana and Bache, obviously! That nincompoop and her obsession with the man who beat her...!"

Kali removed her mask once more and let out a deep sigh. From that, Aiz realized that her guess had been correct, and a bead of sweat trickled down her cheek.

"This is all your fault, you know. Every one of my girls who was bested by one of your menfolk ended up like Argana."

Finally, Aiz realized what had happened. Kali's Amazons had

fallen afoul of their race's characteristic trait—an irresistible attraction toward men who beat them in battle. Argana had shifted from simply lusting for battle to lusting over Finn as well, just the same as Tione had.

Kali and her familia were currently holed up in Port Meren, though more than once, eager Amazons had forced their way into Orario since then.

"Bache was busy doing the ritual, so she's safe," explained Kali. "She and Tiona are probably the only sane Amazons left."

"..."

"Argana's always scared me, but now it's for a completely different reason. Every day, I'm in tears trying to stop her rampage. The other children don't even listen to me..."

"..."

"It's hard on Bache, too. She's got just as much on her plate as I do..."

"...I-I'm sorry..."

"Rrragh! Don't apologize!" said Kali, stamping her feet. "That just makes it worse! It just proves that that washboard goddess managed to get back at me!"

All Aiz could do was watch on, feeling a sense of guilt rise on behalf of Finn and her other male peers. At the same time, however, a strange notion occurred to her.

Until recently, *Kali Familia* had been chasing after Tione and Tiona with the aim of creating the ultimate warrior. How strange it was to be talking so casually with their chief god now, when just a month ago, the two would have naturally been at each other's throats.

"Anyway," said Kali, taking out a Jyaga Maru Kun in one hand. "Now that I get a good look around, Orario sure is a fancy place. There's people and strange wonders as far as the eye can see."

She took a bite of her snack, then noticed Aiz's longing gaze and tossed her a second one.

"Our nation is finished, I tell you. I figured I might as well try to pick up some new blood while I'm here. You wouldn't be interested in a Conversion, would you?"

"I'm not sure if that's…"

"Not even after I gave you a free Jyaga Maru Kun?"

"Ugh…"

Aiz had only taken one bite of her gift and looked like she was about to cough it back up. Seeing her take the bait so seriously, Kali couldn't help but laugh. "Just kidding, just kidding," she said. "Even Ishtar fell to Freya's forces. We were waiting on standby in Port Meren, but now there's nothing for us to do."

"!"

"Guess that damn goddess was more bark than bite…"

Aiz looked up at Kali's words. Noticing her reaction, Kali grinned and waved her hand.

"Sorry, but I don't know anything about this group called the Evils. You're on your own there."

"…"

"Now, then. I guess I'll continue my little sightseeing trip until Bache manages to bring her sister back. Thank you for chatting with me, Sword Princess."

With that, the diminutive deity disappeared into the crowd. Now alone in the commercial district, Aiz peered up at the sky. It was already beginning to darken.

Aiz walked the streets in twilight. It was the border between night and day, and Orario was draped in the last light of the setting sun.

After leaving the commercial district, Aiz decided to make a detour and headed to the southeast end of town. As for why she came here, carrying what she carried, she couldn't say. Perhaps it was because of what happened with Lulune and the members of *Hermes Familia*, or maybe it was due to all those figures from her past whom she had met by chance on the streets today.

In the very same area of town that housed the Pleasure District and Daedalus Street, Aiz came upon her destination.

The First Graveyard, known to some as the Adventurers Graveyard. The multitude of graves in this place memorialized all those who fell in the line of duty, whether it was the Dungeon or war that claimed them and whether their bodies could be retrieved or not.

The sight of the graves brought to mind a terrible longing, almost like homesickness. If she but closed her eyes, Aiz could almost hear the voices of her lost brothers and sisters. She looked down at the bouquet in her hands. It was silent and merely rustled in the wind.

As Aiz walked among the graves, however, she spotted somebody.

"Oh..."

A girl was walking back toward her, having apparently finished her business here. She had smooth raven-black hair and striking crimson eyes. Her clothes were extremely modest pure white garments like the ceremonial robes of a holy priestess. Aiz stood silently, waiting for her to pass, but when the girl got close enough, she turned and acknowledged Aiz's presence.

"It's you..." she said. "Sword Princess."

"Ms. Filvis..."

The elf's eyes widened slightly in genuine surprise but only for a moment. Standing a few paces apart, the two girls stared at each other.

"...This is the first time we've spoken alone," said Filvis at last.

"Yeah..."

"Did you come to lay those flowers?"

"Yeah...Is that...why you're here, too?"

Filvis looked like she was about to nod, but after a moment's thought, she shook her head instead.

"No," she said. "I came here not to give thanks but to apologize."

"..."

Although Aiz had never spoken to Filvis one-on-one before, she had heard the girl's tale from Lefiya.

They called it the Twenty-Seventh-Floor Nightmare. A tragedy orchestrated by the Evils six years prior, in which Filvis had been forced to watch her comrades die. Filvis was the sole survivor of that tragedy, and she had carried the guilt with her ever since.

It was why she called herself unclean.

"...Have you ever felt that fear, Sword Princess?"

"What fear?"

"The fear that one simple mistake could ruin everything."

"..."

"The fear that...you can't save them...That all you can do is watch and be tainted."

Filvis raised her head, directing her blazing crimson eyes into Aiz's own.

"That your very presence is the catalyst for untold tragedy. If you felt that fear, Sword Princess, what would you do?"

This was the question of an elf who had lost everything. Was she trying to say that Aiz was being dragged into a maelstrom of darkness and would be forced to fight her way out? Was it a curse upon Aiz's path or a warning? A word of caution for a dear comrade?

"Would you surrender to your fate? Would you run away? Or... would you stand and fight?"

She posed this question to someone who many considered peerless with the sword. Filvis looked as though she were gazing at a perfect reflection of herself, through the looking glass.

Aiz couldn't answer.

"...I'm sorry," said Filvis. "That was a strange thing to ask."

"No..."

"Good-bye."

With that, Filvis walked past Aiz and left the graveyard. Aiz was left with the girl's question, rattling around in her mind. She turned to watch the girl leave, bathed in the glow of twilight, then resumed her journey.

Aiz ended up in a section of the graveyard reserved for *Loki*

Familia members. Here were buried all the generations of adventurers who came before her, stretching back to Finn, Gareth, and Riveria's time.

Among them were seven graves that looked newer than all the rest. Aiz stepped up to them.

"I'm sorry," she said. "It's been a while, but I'm here."

She placed a single flower at each of the graves, then cast her eyes over the names carved into the headstones. One of them was the name of a healer girl to whom Aiz was much indebted, a girl called Leene Arshe.

She and the six others had lost their lives deep in the bowels of Knossos, the man-made labyrinth, where surviving members of the Evils had been hiding. A dungeon trap had divided the group, and there was nothing Aiz could have done to save them.

Although the scars had healed, the loneliness and grief had turned into a pain that would never go away.

But Aiz wasn't here to repent.

She could not remain fixated on the past. She had to look forward—to keep moving forward, just like Lulune, Asfi, and all of *Hermes Familia* were. To make sure all those wasted lives were not in vain. That was why she had come.

With one half of her face bathed in the dying light, Aiz spoke to her dear, departed comrades.

"I don't even know what I'm supposed to say here," she said. "I'm sorry I failed to protect you."

"It's okay. We don't blame you for it."

"I will keep you in my heart but keep moving forward."

"Please do. We'll always be with you."

"Do you feel angry?"

"Not at all."

"I'll never know."

"I'm sad. Sad I can't go on adventures anymore. Sad I can't be with him anymore."

"Just know that we're all fighting for you now. Even Bete…"
"That makes me so happy. I think I'm going to cry…"
"That's all…I'll see you again."
"We'll be watching over you until then."

Suddenly, Aiz was startled. She felt as if she had just had a conversation with…something. Something very important. It was almost like she could see the girl's smile, hear the girl's voice…like she was right there.

Aiz opened her eyes and spun around. She saw the sea of graves, dyed in the setting sun. She saw the flowers that she and so many other visitors had left.

She was alone. There was no one there. Of course there wasn't.

There was just the wind, ascending into the sky. Aiz stood there for a while, running a hand through her hair, taking it all in.

Then, as she stared at the graves, a voice called out to her.

"Oh? Could that be…? It is! Sword Princess!"

Aiz turned to see a young Amazon.

"Ms. Lena…" she said.

Lena cackled. "Just call me Lena," she said, waving her hand and her ponytail. "We're the same age, aren't we? Are you visiting the graves, too, Sword Princess?"

Lena carried a bouquet of flowers under one arm. Aiz nodded while Lena began placing flowers at the graves by her feet.

They belonged to former members of *Ishtar Familia*—to those brave Amazons who lost their lives in the Evils' cruel hunt.

"The last time I came," said Lena, "it was to tidy up the gravestones. I didn't get time to pay my respects."

"…"

"You know, I bet they'd prefer me bringing booze rather than flowers. But I hope they'll forgive me just this once, because these flowers are my favorite."

Aiz watched as Lena spoke, still looking down at the graves. Each time she laid down one of the pale blue forget-me-nots, Aiz felt the girl's slender fingers imparting some quiet words to the graves themselves.

Eventually, when she was done, Lena stood up and turned around. The light of the sunset was behind her, and she smiled.

"Thank you, Sword Princess."

"What for?"

"Bete Loga and the others told me…Told me about how much you've been fighting for this city…for all of us."

"…"

"Because of you, people like me and Aisha are still alive."

"But…we didn't save so many others."

"Whoa, there! Less of that self-deprecating talk, please! Just accept my words on behalf of the whole city, if you don't mind!"

"…"

"We all want to say…thank you."

She stood there, beautifully illuminated by the light of the setting sun. Aiz felt like she could say nothing, like her chest was growing tight with emotion.

It was like someone was finally saying that her path had been worth it after all. That, even if only for one moment, she was allowed to feel proud.

"I'd better be going," said Lena. "I have to go ask around and find out how many kids Bete Loga wants!"

With a sunny smile, the girl departed. Aiz looked down at her palm, then around at the graves. There were dozens of them, all around. Dozens of tiny monuments to the moments in Aiz's life.

And Aiz swore she could see, as dusk drew in, the path that she had taken. The trails by which she and her allies had arrived at the present moment.

And also the untold paths stretching on to unknown futures. Infinite possibilities that left Aiz feeling lost and stranded.

But then she smiled. From somewhere behind her came the voices of her dearest friends.

"Ms. Aiz! There you are! Filvis told us you'd come this way!"

"Why didn't you tell us? We all could have come with you, you know."

"And who invited Bete anyway? Did he really need to come along?"

"Who said I needed your permission, dumbass? If you don't like me, then piss off!"

"Hey!!"

"Settle down, please. Do not disturb the souls of all who rest here."

"Oh dear, and here I thought the three of us could visit our fallen friends in peace."

"Gah-hah-hah! You should know by now, Finn, that our familia does nothing in peace!"

"Damn right! And I bet my kids are lookin' down at us from heaven right now and smilin'!"

These were the voices of her friends. The friends who had saved her life on so many occasions.

They gave Aiz the courage to walk this path to its conclusion, wherever that might be.

Because of them, she wasn't alone.

The girl's friends hurried over to her and gathered beneath the dusklight while all the souls of all the heroes watched from their jet-black monuments, eager to see what kind of Oratoria these girls would write.

MIRAGE IN A SEA OF SAND

A shallow slumber envelops me.
 I linger on the border of sleep and wakefulness, hounded by the same old thoughts.
 Am I a good king? Am I taking those silver teachings to heart?
 Can I present myself proudly to the woman who taught me?
 Lady Ali...Lady Ali...
 My mind rocks as if in a cradle. Even the voice calling my name sounds distant and faint.
 Oh, where am I? *When* am I?

"King Aram!"

The voice rouses me from slumber. I slowly open my eyes to see the stout face of the merchant man who has been my stalwart ally through all my joys and sorrows.
 "...Bofman?"
 "Yes, it's me, Your Majesty. Are you all right? You seem tired," remarks Bofman, seeing me stare off into space. "The party is about to begin. You shall be representing our fledgling nation out there. The people will be very keen to see how the young king of Shalzad conducts himself."
 "...Ah, yes, you're right. Apologies. I think I slept too much last night."
 Whipping my idle brain to work, I stand up from my chair.

Many moons have passed since the end of the Calamity of the Hot Sands, the war between Shalzad and Warsa. Plenty of time for a naive, young girl to blossom into an adult, whether she wants to or not, and for a weak prince to mature into a brilliant king.

Shalzad has become arguably the first great nation to rise from the vast swathes of the west-central region of the Kaios Desert. This founding is what the upcoming gathering purports to commemorate…but in reality, it is little more than an opportunity for rival states to determine our influence. Representatives from every neighboring state will be attending with the sole purpose of probing me for weakness and assessing where they fit into the new balance of power.

"It has been a long road, Bofman. Thank you for accompanying me this far."

"Not at all, Your Majesty. We of the Fazoul Trading Company simply spotted a business opportunity and capitalized on it."

Bofman has lost a lot of weight since I first met him and distanced himself from his moneymaking habits. Now he is the very model of a dignified statesman, and while I do not know what possessed him to receive a Falna and level up twice, I do know that Shalzad would not be half the nation it is today without his tireless service.

Even I have grown a little taller, something I thought I would never see. With age comes wisdom and the broadening of my horizons. I can scarcely imagine making the same, ignorant remarks today that I made back then.

We have all grown much since that day. Myself, Bofman, all of us.

"…I thank each of you for coming all this way today. It may only be for a short time, but I welcome you. Wise people of distant lands, I pray the desert watches over you all."

After stepping into the main hall and greeting the guests with a speech that could charitably be described as "not boring," the grand ball is underway. There is wine and flowers, dance, and the graceful, plucked tones of the oud. A celebration of Shalzad's rich culture.

Most of the hushed voices I overhear are centered around me.
"So that's King Aram…"
"He really is as handsome as the rumors say."
"That and his shrewdness make for an impressive package."
"Did the gods not mistakenly bless him with too many gifts?"
"Oh, I wonder if he would grace me with a dance?"

In the crowd, I spot the prime minister of the largest empire in the world; the top mage of Altina, kingdom of magic; nobility from Dizara, the ocean realm that is the opposite of the sandy lands of Kaios in every way; and even representatives of Orario, the Labyrinth City…Although I am a leader myself, I reel at the thought of meeting these dignitaries face-to-face. Even something as minor as the order in which I greet them can be taken as an affront. It is no exaggeration to say that my actions represent those of Shalzad itself, and just as one good word can secure the future of my nation, one ill-timed remark can seal its fate.

I begin making acquaintances, at times showing deference, and at others projecting strength, until at last, just as I am approaching the end of my first round of introductions, I come across a lively group.

"Princess! You mustn't stuff your face when there are people watching!"

"But, Uskali, the food here is amazing! You try some, too, Lidari!"

"I'll pass. I don't mean to be rude, but the cuisine of this country does not agree with my tastes."

A strikingly beautiful princess, accompanied by an elf and a blindfolded swordsman who appear to be her escorts. They are each enjoying the delectable culinary delights our humble nation has to offer.

As I approach, the princess, clearly a blend of multiple heritages, calls out to me.

"Oh, it's the king! Hello! Pleased to meet you!"

"A pleasure to make your acquaintance, Princess Talvi," I say. "Are you enjoying the festivities?"

"Yes!" she beams. "Thank you for inviting us to such a wonderful event! But are you sure it wasn't a mistake? Our country's just some backwater village, you know?"

"Princess! You mustn't address His Majesty so carelessly! Nor should you heap shame upon Beltane like that!"

"But it's true," the princess replies. "We're just nestled in the mountains somewhere. It's basically not even a country at all!"

"Princess…!"

The elf, apparently a long-suffering attendant to the princess, groans and clutches his head. The swordsman, meanwhile, seems utterly unconcerned with anything besides the princess's safety. They make for such an amusing trio that I can't help but smile. The bonds of familiahood run deep—even I can see that.

"Princess Talvi," I say. "Rest assured, your presence here is no mistake. I would very much like to ask about the secret waters that your nation is said to conceal."

"Oh, that's what this is about! Okay, sure! I don't mind!"

Despite her graceful appearance, Princess Talvi can be surprisingly childish. Charming and expressive, she paints quite a stark contrast to a certain overburdened little girl, weighed down by royal duty. Her bright and gentle smile brings happiness to everyone who lays eyes on her.

"By the way," she says. "I saw how you handled Orario just now. I can't believe you beat back that big bully and got a good deal out of it!"

"Ha-ha…You must have been watching. Apologies if you saw me acting a little above my station," I say, picking my words carefully so as not to cause offense to any involved party. It seems the princess bore witness to my now-signature negotiation style.

The nations of Kaios have become increasingly dependent on trade with Altena in recent years, such as for the construction of the desert ships. I have been speaking with the head of Orario's Guild, who is very keen to agree to a trade deal on magic stones instead.

What I proposed was essentially a student exchange program. The idea was that I would promote magic-stone trade as much as possible, but in return, I would be allowed to send several of Shalzad's top warriors to train in Orario—specifically, within the Dungeon.

The harsh desert environment of Kaios is famous for producing many second-tier adventurers called *kavir*. Even Aisha Belka of the Berbera found her start among these dunes. We thus had a great number of diamonds in the rough without any means of refining them.

I suggested that Orario take these fledgling warriors and train them, and in the future, they could even join Orario's familias, thus bolstering the standing armies of the Labyrinth City. In return, however, they would be obligated to take on quests to further the long-term benefit of our nation.

I know from firsthand experience how devastating an adventurer can be. It is only natural, then, that I seek to harness that power for the sake of my homeland. If Orario refused, then that was their prerogative. It would simply mean that I would have sent my countrymen to Altina to learn magic instead. When I presented this alternative, there was much handwringing from Mr. Mardeel, but in the end, he accepted my proposal.

It is always nice when either outcome of a negotiation is desirable. I think back to the elf who taught me that.

"But there's one thing I don't get," says the princess. "How come you call yourself a king and not a queen?"

As soon as she says that, I freeze. Fortunately, none of the other partygoers seem to have heard her. Even her own attendants simply tilt their heads and ask, "Princess? What are you talking about?" By my side, I hear Jafar's breath catch in his throat, and I think poor Bofman nearly died.

...Perhaps I am not giving this princess the credit she deserves. I considered her a childish, naive individual, but she is apparently quite perceptive.

In the awkward silence that follows, I rack my brains thinking how best to respond, when all of a sudden, the music changes. Now it is time for the second part of my ball, an interlude in the continental style.

Seizing the serendipitous change of mood, I smile at the princess and offer my hand.

"You have piqued my interest, Your Highness. Would you care for a dance?"

"Oh, so Shalzad doesn't allow queens. I'm sorry. I didn't know..."

We walk up the steps, hand in hand, as elegant music plays.

Knowing I can't keep secrets, I decide to tell Princess Talvi everything about the circumstances of my birth and my country. When I finish, the princess looks genuinely ashamed.

It attracts a great number of stares from the other dignitaries to see a king dancing with a princess of a foreign nation, but there is little I can do about that, save keep a smile on my face and ensure my voice remains hushed.

"I thought maybe you were hurting yourself for everyone else as well...That's why I asked."

She means no harm; I can see that. But I notice something else.

"As well."

"What do you mean by that?" I ask.

"In the past, I sacrificed my own well-being for the sake of my country," the princess explains. "I was so, so scared, but I didn't want anyone else to worry, so I smiled and pretended it was fine."

I don't know what she's been through, but what I heard shocks me.

"Ever since I first saw you," she says, "I thought you and I might be the same."

I can't help but agree with that sentiment.

"It's true that I did that once," I reply. "I saw myself as a stepping stone. A figurehead to keep the throne warm and my people happy."

I have been content to do as my father wishes, to conceal my gender and offer myself up for the good of my nation. That isn't what Ali wants. I have been forcing myself to be Aram instead.

But...

"I'm not like that anymore."

Today, I smile with my whole heart. No longer am I resigned to walk the path fate has drawn for me.

"I love this country and all the people who live here."

"!"

"There have been hard times. On more than one occasion have I considered sacrificing myself for my country. But through it all, I have never resented my people, and I trust the same is true for you as well."

The princess's eyes, colored like two different gemstones, fly wide-open.

"Because a passing goddess once told me that sacrifice...is the most meaningless death of all. Instead, I have decided to lead my countrymen in my own way. To guide them."

"'To guide them'?"

"Yes. To have faith in myself and to show my people the way...like a true hero."

I think back on the words that now provide such a deep foundation for my life. At first, the princess is silent, but then...

"...That's right. You're so right. Just like Bell and Haruhime!"

Her cheeks redden, and she smiles like a child. Just then, the music comes to an end. I marvel at how well we came to understand one another in such a short time.

We still our steps and smile at each other, and then the princess speaks, looking up ever so slightly into my eyes.

"I think I like you, Aram. I really do."

I am surprised to hear that at first, but it slowly dawns on me that here is a soul that treasures each encounter like no other.

However, her words immediately throw the room into uproar, with onlookers taking them as either a declaration of love or an amorous proposition. I do not enjoy being the bearer of bad news, but I fear such dreams are doomed from the start.

"I feel the same way," I reply. "Glad am I to have met you, Talvi."

Thus, our miraculous meeting comes to a close, with me addressing the princess on a first-name basis, as she has done with me. I watch as she waves and vanishes into the crowd, giving thanks to fate for arranging this dreamlike encounter.

However, as I stand there, still feeling the effects of our conversation, a voice from behind breaks me out of my reverie.

"Excuse me, Your Majesty. Could I bother you for a moment of your time?"

When I turn, I am treated to yet another shock, for standing there is a prum gentleman I know well.

"My name is Finn Deimne," the man says. "A humble adventurer from Orario…Alas, not so humble as to require further introduction, I fear."

He is confident but not incorrect. This man is the captain of *Loki Familia*, one of the most powerful organizations in the world. No doubt he is here accompanying Orario's representative, Mr. Mardeel.

"A first-tier adventurer from the Labyrinth City," I say. "You honor me with your presence, Mr. Deimne."

I then turn my attention to the girl by his side, who curtsies politely.

"…Pleased to meet you, Your Majesty. My name is Aiz Wallenstein."

If I am to be perfectly frank, the girl's beauty instantly steals my breath away. Why, she is very nearly an equal to a goddess of beauty herself. Certainly, the fairest face at the gathering by far.

She has been blessed with the youthful appearance of a girl just sixteen summers, though by no means childish, and while I wonder how much of that is caused by her falna, I notice that every pair of eyes in proximity, whether man or woman, is drawn to her captivating looks. She seems like a nymph that has just stepped out of a fairy-tale book.

After I regain my composure, I return her soft and gentle smile with my own.

"I wasn't intending to get involved in all these politics," says Finn. "We're just the muscle, you see…But I must admit, something about you intrigues me."

I feel the man's discerning eye look me up and down, then he looks at me and grins.

"Would you indulge me in a game of Halvan?" he asks.

"You mean…right now?"

"If you wouldn't mind. I'd like to test your mettle."

I can't believe what I am hearing. Surely even Mr. Deimne knows of my skill at the game. While he produces a *malik* out of thin air and begins twiddling it in his fingers, Ms. Wallenstein grows visibly distressed.

"…Are you sure about this, Finn?" she asks.

"Not really. Go keep Royman occupied for me, would you?"

Finn turns his eyes to me and grins a fearless smile.

"I'm going to give a desert king his just *deserts*."

So this is the famed Braver. He is a little cheekier than I was expecting, but I am happy to accept. For my part, I have been humiliated at Orario's hands before—specifically by those of a certain goddess of beauty and her followers. I am long overdue for a little payback.

"Very well," I say. "I relish the opportunity to teach Braver something for a change."

In short order, a board is set up in a corner of the room. Jafar is none too pleased—saying this is hardly the time or the place to be playing games—but I try my best to ignore him. After all, the night promises to be replete with politics. What is the harm in a little diversion? I argue the visiting dignitaries are surely getting bored by now and that a little stimulation will do them all good.

"Do you know how to play, Mr. Deimne?"

"I've been reading up on it from the moment I set foot in these lands. You don't need to worry on that front."

Is that really enough to grasp the essentials of such a complex game? He reminds me of a goddess I use to know.

It has been a long time since my competitive spirit reared its head, and despite my best efforts, I can't stop my lips from curling into a grin.

"I'm afraid I mustn't keep people waiting. Would you mind if we try to keep this quick?"

"Go right ahead."

I throw down the gauntlet right from the get-go, just as I had on that one fated occasion all that time ago.

And the similarities, if I had anything to say about it, will not end there.

"...Regicide?!"

Everyone around us, including Finn, gasps. I invoked the rule of sacrifice, passing the *malik* status to my own *malika*.

Of course, it is just a game, but people immediately begin speculating on my intentions. What did I mean by committing such a symbolic move?

Well, I'm sorry to be a spoilsport, but I didn't mean anything by it. If it was a slight, then it was one only a certain goddess living in Orario would understand.

As the implications of my unconventional move sink in, Finn smiles and presses his own assault.

"...It's my loss."

It was practically a game of Blitz Halvan. Finn required no time at all to consider his moves, yet trapped my *malika* quite magnificently. The game lasted around two hundred moves, and while all the onlookers cooed in delight, I was left feeling completely drained.

"It's been too long since I last played a game," I say. "I had hoped to secure victory, but it seems it wasn't in the stars."

All my efforts to mimic a goddess have gone to waste. I exhale a deep sigh.

"I'm sure you might have won had you stuck to a more orthodox playstyle," says Finn. "Plus"—he carefully reverts the board to a state approximately fifty moves prior—"if you moved your *merkabah* here instead of your *rauch*, then I would have lost."

"What?!"

"Amazing!"

"He came that close to beating Braver?!"

The crowd begins to murmur. I, on the other hand, am struck by the queer feeling—this is not the first time I have been humbled in this manner. Perhaps I placed too much stock in teachings I still don't fully understand. All I can see in my mind's eye is an elf and a catman, jeering at me.

"...I always seem to let victory slip my grasp at the most crucial moment," I mutter. Wearing a wry smile, I begin to collect the pieces, while the spectators offer a polite smattering of applause and file away one-by-one.

"Still, I'm a little surprised," I say, once only Finn and I remain.

"By what, Your Majesty?"

"I never took you for such a clean player."

All is fair in love and Halvan. In our game, whenever Finn made a sacrifice, I would make moves to provoke him. I was mostly interested to see whether he would choose to play dirty or not.

From what I know of Finn Deimne, morals mean little to him. He is a man willing to do whatever it takes to achieve his aims, whether that means pulling tricks or making sacrifices. A true statesman, like one of us.

However, the Finn I played against was not like that at all. He never hesitated to make the fair and upright choice every single time.

"I always thought you were more willing to get your hands dirty," I say.

"Well, you aren't wrong," replies Finn, unoffended by my unflattering preconception. "If that's what's required of me, then I will. This is...a little embarrassing to admit, but there was a time I considered myself a man-made hero. It wasn't until fairly recently that I realized just how meaningless that title was."

"What happened?"

"A group of heretics and a young boy happened. In that turmoil... I saw the light."

Finn smiles.

"An imitation, no matter how perfect it is, will never be real," he says. "I realized that what I was lacking was strength, conviction... and ambition. So now, I walk the high road."

Finn's words cut much deeper than I expect. Long ago, I struggled to accept whether I was qualified to lead. Has the man before me gone through that struggle as well?

"And it's not just me who's changed," says Finn. "Aiz has, too, though I'm not sure whether it's for the same reason or not."

I follow Finn's gaze, to see the golden-haired girl conversing cheerfully with Princess Talvi.

In all honesty, I have been thinking the same ever since she curtsied before me. The girl is far more amicable than her nickname, "Doll Princess," led me to believe. People call the Sword Princess an instrument of destruction, an avatar of slaughter, but perhaps she, too, has come up against her own troubles and found her own answers.

I look out across the resplendent hall, taking in the party atmosphere, when a somber mood takes hold of me.

"Mr. Deimne," I ask. "Are you handling Mr. Mardeel's security by yourselves? What of the other great faction of Orario? ...Are they not here?"

I was half hoping to spot that whimsical goddess. Maybe she snuck into the party or sent her followers to check on me. To see how I've grown.

Maybe…Maybe……

My own desperation disgusts me.

"I'm afraid it's just us," says Finn. "Well, there is another familia helping, but…Ah, that's right. Now that you mention it, Lady Freya did ask me to pass along a message to the king of Shalzad."

"!"

I lift my head, and Finn imparts the contents of that message to me. "She says, 'I have found my Odr.'"

"Haruhime! It's been so long!"

"Princess Talvi! I missed you so very much!"

I watch as two foreign princesses clasp hands and giggle together. Meanwhile, I approach the boy who is standing nearby.

"It's a pleasure to make your acquaintance, Mr. Bell Cranell."

"O-oh, Your Majesty! Pleased to meet you!"

Surrounded by a baby-faced goddess and his other friends, the white-haired adventurer gives a hurried bow.

He lacks any of the dignity that Finn and Aiz possess. So much so that I wonder if this is really the boy I have been told about.

To be honest, I am jealous of him. Between the two of us, I am the more handsome one by far, and he seems perpetually nervous, like a young child. How could someone like him have stolen that goddess's heart? I peer into his clear, rubellite eyes—the eyes of a hero—and speak.

"I have heard tales of your many adventures," I say. "I would like to ask you something, if you don't mind. How is it that you have been able to overcome all the trials along your path?"

The boy doesn't hesitate.

"Because of all the people I've met," he says, wearing a proud smile. "They've helped me and taught me so much. It's only because of them that I'm here today."

The goddess by his side grins. His friends all smile warmly for a boy who will never change.

"I have to pay them back for all the times they've saved me," he says. "That's the only reason I've come so far."

It is white. Blindingly white.

So this is the hero to the downtrodden.

I see it now, Freya. It was this blinding, clear sparkle that stole your heart. You always were susceptible to it.

I chuckle to myself at the thought.

"Mr. Cranell," I say. "I would very much like to hear more tales of your adventures, if you wouldn't mind."

What I want is very simple.

"I would like to know the path a hero walks."

This is a meeting of many people. An intersection of many roads. Many stories.

A desert king, a snow princess, a hero with secret ambitions, a sword honed through battle, and a savior of many others. Today, all are present on this sea of sand.

As I marvel over just how miraculous this meeting is, I…

"Lady Ali!"

The moment I hear those words, I know my dream is over.

"…Bofman."

"Yes, it's me, my lady. Are you all right? You seem tired."

They were the very same words I heard at the start of my dream, but the place and time are completely different.

I am in the royal palace of Shalzad, and as I look around, I see that Jafar is there. My retainers are as well. They are all there to look after me, the young prince.

"The Warsa army may be in retreat," says Bofman, "but this is where our battles truly begin. The restoration of Shalzad will be an onerous task…This is where we shall see if Lady Freya is truly watching over you."

Bofman kneels in deference. From his behavior, I can tell it was shortly after the goddess and her followers departed from these lands.

As I sit atop a throne only recently won back, a smile spreads across my lips.

"...I had a dream," I say.

As I try to remember, I find the contents of my dream turning to white, and after a few moments, I can no longer recall who I talked to or what we discussed. All that stays with me now are feelings of joy and love.

"Our nation was thriving, and I had become its glorious king, introducing myself on the world stage..."

"Th-this is surely a portentous sign! A blessing upon you and your reign, Lady Ali!"

By my side, Jafar grins a wide smile.

Is this dream prophecy or delusion? I can't possibly know that yet. Even if I stay the course, how can I be sure that the paths of the people I met in it will ever intersect with mine? How can I be sure that the stories I heard will remain the same?

They might not.

When I approach, the reality may end up being quite different.

But even so, I will hold this mirage close to my heart.

I will have faith in myself and conduct myself with dignity, like a hero. All so that I may meet those people again.

"Now, then," I say. "Let us begin."

And so I start down the path of my story, but a single thread of a rich tapestry.

GIRLS×CROSS: FOUR PATHS OF A HALF YEAR

"Look, Lefiya, look! They just released this week's adventurer rankings!"

Elfie, Lefiya's roommate, came bounding through the door, a stack of parchments in her hands. Until today, Lefiya had been forcing herself to undergo harsh training, but Riveria had ordered her to take a break, so today, she was recuperating with a large pot of freshly boiled tea at her side.

Amid had secretly lent her a book on magical healing, and Lefiya was making her way through it. Admittedly, this stretched the definition of a day off, but at least Lefiya's body was getting the rest it needed, and spending the day not doing anything at all would have been even more damaging…At least, that was how Lefiya rationalized it.

The ascension to Level 5 of a certain bothersome bunny also weighed on her mind, as it meant Lefiya had finally been overtaken. This brought a renewed sense of motivation, albeit in the *Just you wait, I'll murder you* way.

Several months had passed since the Enyo incident, and Lefiya was no longer in such a rush as she was before to improve. Instead, she worked more carefully and diligently, while still making sure to further her efforts every single day.

Elfie, of course, remained quite ignorant of all this, being more interested in trend-chasing and gossip than her own studies.

"The War Game was quite a while ago now," she said, "but it still seems to be affecting the rankings! Seems like things got shaken up while I wasn't looking!"

She slammed the pile of parchment onto Lefiya's desk, causing the sheets to scatter across her open book.

"*Sigh*...Can't you see I'm reading?" Lefiya groaned. "I don't want to get into all this."

"C'mon! We haven't done this in *ages*! I haven't been able to keep up-to-date because I've been looking after you, you know?"

"Urgh..."

"Let's go through them together! It'll be fun!"

Elfie's resentful comment, followed swiftly by her unbridled enthusiasm, left Lefiya with no room to respond. Instead, she sighed again and agreed to her roommate's demands.

"And as we all know, same as always, at the top of the 'Greatest Female Adventurer' list is Aiz! ...Psych! It's Riveria this time! I guess officially reaching Level Seven was big for her!"

"No surprises there. Numerically speaking, Level Seven is a monumental achievement, but from an adventurer's point of view, she is a mage and, thus, needs protection in battle, unlike Aiz who can fight alone. It doesn't make sense to compare them, and quite frankly, any comparison is nonsense. If, heaven forbid, they were to fight each other, the outcome would be entirely determined by the lay of the land and other strategic considerations. So Aiz is by no means inferior, but the reverse is true as well, and in addition to her peerless sorcery, Riveria also bears the crown of high elf royalty and carries the entire dignity of our race with her."

"Wow, this is only the first one, and you're already getting into it..."

Seeing her roommate casually rattle off an entire long-form chant, Elfie was understandably astounded.

"You're geeking out about Riveria getting first place, but you also don't want to stop repping Aiz. Must be tough fangirling for two, huh?"

Lefiya blushed and cleared her throat as if to change the subject.

Still, she didn't quite understand some of the words Elfie was saying. That girl had been hanging around the gods a little too much lately.

"Well, Riveria came out on top in the all-inclusive Mage Rankings, too!" Elfie went on. "But it was a close match between her and Hildsleif! If Riveria hadn't clinched that level up, she'd be in a real sticky spot!"

"That just goes to show how impactful the War Game was," Lefiya replied. "Even a fellow mage like myself was surprised at how radically his deeds shifted the flow of battle."

"The 'Greatest Female Adventurer' poll was really close, too! Someone tied with Aiz for second place, and third place was only two votes behind! In second place was Mia Grand from the Benevolent Mistress, and third was Lyu, that mysterious elf! That masked adv*eleon*…Just who could she b*eleon*?"

"What in the world are you even saying, Elfie? *Sigh*…I was hoping that with Tiona and Tione on our side, *Loki Familia* could keep the top four spots all to ourselves as usual, but I suppose it's not to be… As you say, it seems like we'll be seeing the aftereffects of the War Game for quite some time…"

"You got that right. It's actually kind of amazing that Aiz managed to hang in there. I guess the Sword Princess's brand recognition is just too strong!"

"The Hyrutes only came to Orario five years ago, whereas Aiz lived through the Age of Darkness and was already famous because of that. That's a difficult gap to close…"

For all her earlier protests, once the conversation got started, Lefiya couldn't help herself and immediately joined in. Enjoying the excitement and chattiness teen girls were famous for, Elfie smiled and pulled out another sheet.

"Now, ladies and gentlemen, it's the one you've all been waiting for! It's time to announce the Top Female Mage Rankings! And our very own Lefiya comes in—drum roll please—wow! An astounding fourth place!"

"Hm."

"Come on! Show a little emotion, why don't you? You were so excited when you heard about Aiz!"

"I just don't have time to work myself into a tizzy over some popularity contest."

"You're so boring these days! What happened to the adorable Lefiya who goes, 'Oh…hee-hee…me? I'm still not that good…'?!"

"Please don't make fun of me…no matter how accurate it may or may not be."

Lefiya shot Elfie a rotten glare, which caused the girl to break into crocodile tears.

"Oh, my dear Lefiya's changed so much—it's like I barely know her anymore! *Sob, sob!*"

"I'm not *your* Lefiya. Besides, we all change; that's what makes us mortal."

"Ooh, look at you, getting all philosophical…Fine! Let's just look at some more rankings, then! …Hmm. You know, everywhere I look, Aiz seems to be somewhere in the top ten. Riveria and the Hyrutes, too. I think it's always been like that."

"Well, of course. They're all very impressive women."

"You said it. Our familia, especially the girls, seems to be topping every—Wait, WHAAAAAAT?? Rabbit Foot beat Aiz in something?!"

Lefiya nearly choked on her tea before emitting a shrill shriek. "What?! Show me that!!"

"Right here! In the 'City's Fastest' ranking! Usually it goes Vana Freya, Bete, Aiz, but Rabbit Foot somehow got second place, pushing Aiz out of the top three! What did Bete do to deserve this?!"

"Ridiculous! Preposterous! What are they thinking?" screeched Lefiya, snatching the parchments from Elfie's hands and glaring at them hard enough to burn holes in the paper. "How could that philandering human possibly be faster than Ms. Aiz?! He's only Level Five! Don't they know Aiz is Level Six?! If she uses her magic, there's no way he can keep up! How dare he come in second?! Doesn't he know his place? Just who does he think he is?!"

You're way madder about him beating Aiz than you were about him overtaking you...

"I bet it's all because of that final sprint during the War Game, but that was only thanks to all the magical buffs he had! It shouldn't count! It's ridiculous! Ri! Di! Cu! Lous! It's made me so angry I can't even talk right! This is why I can't stand the brainwashed masses!"

Weren't you also cheering quite hard at the time...?

While Elfie crossed her arms and adopted a meditative silence, Lefiya kept going through the rankings until she received a second shock.

"And not just the 'City's Fastest,' but look here! In the 'Most Handsome Human' ranking, Aiz is fourteenth place, and Bell Cranell is thirteenth! How could he beat her not once but twice?! S-something's wrong!! This just isn't riiiiiiiiiight!!"

"What's not right is that Aiz is in those rankings, Lefiya...It's supposed to be for men, but I guess Loki made Aiz dress up as a man in the past, and that left such a strong impression that people are still thinking about it..."

"No! I refuse to accept it! These rankings aren't fair! There's corruption afoot, I tell you! We must rise up and oppose this villainy and put society back on track with a fair, balanced survey that accurately represents the *truth* of this world!"

"W-wait, Lefiya?!"

Before Elfie could stop her, Lefiya stormed out into the hallway. Elfie stood there frozen, arm outstretched, before finally relaxing into a sweet smile.

"Lefiya," she said. "It's good to see you haven't changed that much after all..."

Lefiya was furious.

This rabbit was wicked and cruel, ignorant and uneducated, and brazen and unscrupulous. Lefiya was determined to eliminate him at all costs.

As a good little elf girl, Lefiya didn't know much about the rankings. She just sang her songs and obliterated her monsters. But when it came to the rabbit, she was far more attentive to him than anybody else in the city.

"I simply can't believe that human could ever catch up to Ms. Aiz! I have to get these rankings retracted! And if I catch sight of that rabbit in the meantime, I'll *Arcs Ray* him into next week!"

Lefiya had dashed out of the Twilight Manor and made her way down Main Street, her goal being to find out who was responsible for these rankings and have their license revoked. While it was primarily the entertainment-starved gods who organized them, Lefiya had heard that the volunteers who did the canvassing were allowed to come up with their own categories. Her top priority, then, was to seek out and apprehend whatever sick, twisted individual was responsible for pushing heretical rabbit worship among the unwashed masses.

But Orario is a big place. How am I supposed to track down one person in this massive city...?

"Excuse me, ladies and gentlemen? Would anyone like to take part in a survey? It's called the 'Best, Greatest, and Cutest Fourteen-Year-Old Male Adventurer with White Hair!'"

"That's them!!!!"

Lefiya immediately homed in on the lunatic she was searching for after they conveniently exposed themselves.

"Halt right there, criminal scum!" she yelled. "What sort of questionnaire is this supposed to be?!"

"Oh, this?" the culprit replied with an innocent tilt of the head. "It's just my own personalized cheat category that I crafted solely and specially so that only my dear Bell could possibly win it."

"Talk about saying the quiet part out loud!! Are you all right in the head?! ...Wait, don't I *know* who you are...?"

Lefiya paused. The slanderer turned out to be a pretty young girl with blue-gray hair, and she was wearing an apron over a green uniform that Lefiya knew well.

"You're from The Benevolent Mistress," she said. "Syr Flover, was it...?"

"What a coincidence, running into each other on the streets like this."

With a bundle of parchments under one arm, Syr smiled. It was so clearly the smile of a sweet, innocent city girl that Lefiya didn't know how to respond. Very quickly, however, her sense of justice spurred her on.

"Ms. Flover!" she demanded. "What are you up to?!"

"Please, call me Syr," she replied. "And allow me to call you Ms. Lefiya in turn. Now, would you mind telling me what this is all about?"

"...All right then, Ms. Syr!" Beneath the clear blue sky, in the center of the main road, Lefiya thrust her finger at Syr. "I hereby accuse you of attempting to whitewash the sinful deeds of a lecherous human, while simultaneously manipulating the public opinion of good, upstanding adventurers like Ms. Aiz! I demand you put a stop to this slanderous survey, right now!"

"Wow, such passion!" replied Syr with affected surprise. "You remind me of a certain attendant I know!"

Syr's lackluster reaction took the wind out of Lefiya's sails and caused her to reflect on her behavior just a little. The girl was little more than an acquaintance, and yet here Lefiya was, lambasting her with accusations in the middle of the street. It just wasn't the elven way. Lefiya took a moment to recompose herself, then launched into a more evenhanded interrogation.

"So what has possessed you to act in this way, Ms. Syr?"

"I was forced into it," said Syr, suddenly dejected, "as penance for losing the War Game. All the gods and goddesses hate me now, so they made me go around doing these surveys. Boo-hoo..."

Syr drew her sleeve across her face and spilled a few crocodile tears in her defense. Lefiya, meanwhile, arched her slender eyebrows. It wasn't immediately obvious to her why a simple waitress had to pay the price for *Freya Familia*'s loss.

That was because Lefiya and the rest of *Loki Familia* had been underground on an expedition at the time of Freya's little plot, and it was only upon returning to the surface, long after everything had been decided, that she found out what had gone on in their absence. When she returned, Lefiya was baffled to find the *Hestia* and *Freya Familias* already gearing up for war. Hence, with the exception of a few people and the gods themselves, no one in the city knew about the connection between Syr and Freya.

Instead, Lefiya assumed that the girl must be some kind of non-adventurer member of *Freya Familia* and left it at that. It wasn't Syr's situation that bothered her right now.

"I understand...Enough to see your plight, at least," she said. "However, Ms. Syr, I must ask that you cease and desist this blatant manipulation of public opinion at once!"

"Okay, then! You're right; it is a little obvious, isn't it? Then how about this one? Would you like to cast your vote for the 'Super-Duper Record Holder Who Leaves All the Other Rankings in the Dust'?!"

"Are you even listening to me...?"

Without a shred of malice about her, Syr had whipped out a category that was even more explosive than the last. Lefiya's fists began to shake. She had thought there was something oddly stubborn about the girl when she first saw her at the bar, almost as if she were a demon toying with gods and mortals alike, but she didn't expect anything like this!

"But the gods stuck me with this job," Syr protested, "so if I don't do it right, they'll get mad at me!"

"I don't think they told you to ask such ridiculous questions, did they?!"

"Oh, they did. But it's mostly just because I want to!"

"Grhhhhhhhhh!!"

For the first time in her spotless life, Lefiya was driven by the urge to slap another person. She had to clutch her right hand with her left to stop it leaping up on its own.

"Why," she screamed, with all the force of an erupting volcano, "are you so obsessed with this boy Bell Cranell?!"

"Because I like him."

Lefiya stopped breathing. Syr's honest answer, delivered alongside a genuine smile, was the polar opposite of her behavior so far.

"It's not for his sake that I'm doing this; it's for my own. I want to know how this city feels about him. I want to learn all about him, all the things I never knew before. Maybe by doing that…I can do something about this love in my heart…Perhaps I'll drive myself crazy…but that, too, will be my punishment."

Like that of a goddess, this ordinary town girl gave a benevolent smile. Like a nun seeking penance for her crimes or a child hiding their secrets away in a drawer, Syr gripped the parchments and squeezed them close to her chest.

Lefiya stood there, dumbfounded, as her ears turned vermilion. Syr's words embarrassed her far more than the girl herself.

As the elf girl shook her head left and right to rid herself of the sour feeling in her stomach, Syr took the opportunity to ask her a question in return.

"How do you feel about Bell, Ms. Lefiya?"

"Wha—? Th-that human? I…I…couldn't care less!"

"But it's because of him that you're out here, isn't it? Whatever you may think of him, it must be very powerful indeed. What is it?"

The time for opening her own heart had passed, and the smile on Syr's lips returned to its former state. Lefiya let out a trapped groan.

She was seething with anger. Not because Syr's words had hit the bull's-eye, but because they weren't too far off from the truth, either. The reason Lefiya couldn't stand Bell overtaking Aiz in the rankings was because it was completely disrespectful to the girl he was supposed to be looking up to. At least, that was the excuse Lefiya went with.

What do I think of that licentious human...?

Lefiya instinctively opened her mouth to deliver a double-spread-worthy rant—a long-form chant no shorter than those of the attendants to the gods that Syr knew—touching on the many times the boy had wronged her, including when he peeped on her and Aiz in the baths and—in what was now Lefiya's most traumatic memory—when he splattered a vial of virility potion all over her hair. Instead, however, she closed her eyes and pondered.

She felt like she was being tested.

Tested by something akin to a god.

And so Lefiya wandered the forest of her thoughts, and after a while, she opened her eyes.

Before them were the blue-gray irises of her interlocutor.

"He's...my rival," she said.

Slightly but surely, those blue-gray eyes widened.

"So...I won't lose," she declared. "Not to Ms. Aiz and not to Bell Cranell, either."

The light of determination flickered to life within her deep blue eyes, and her hair, cut short these days, fluttered gently in the wind.

Syr's momentary surprise was quickly swept away by the hustle and bustle of the street.

Instead, a soft smile appeared on her lips.

"Your soul," she said, "is quite beautiful, too."

"Hm?"

"A radiant amber, like the sun...but also different."

Syr spoke of Lefiya's praises to no one in particular. She closed her eyes.

"I wonder what would have happened," she said, "if you had been the one Hedin brought...There is no point in entertaining what-if's, but I can't help but be curious..."

Lefiya started to wonder what the girl was talking about. But just as she was about to ask, she noticed something.

All around her in the street, people had stopped and were staring—merchants, ordinary citizens, and even gods and goddesses all paused whatever they were doing and watched on with curious gazes, as though something very strange was happening.

Sensing that the unwanted attention was making Lefiya nervous, Syr smiled.

"Now, then," she said. "Ms. Lefiya, would you like to come with me and make sure I don't ask any more inappropriate questions?"

"Huh...?"

"For I'm quite sure I understand how you feel now, Ms. Lefiya!"

Syr gave a big smile.

"Let us roam these streets together and find out what the rest of the city thinks, shall we?"

Lefiya's short time off was shaping up to be a rather unconventional day.

"Sword Princess?"

It happened when Aiz was making her usual visit to the Jyaga Maru Kun stands, touring the city with a bag in her hands. As she made her way down Southwest Main Street, a female voice called out to her.

"It's you...From The Benevolent Mistress..."

Each stopped and turned their head over their shoulders, locking eyes in the middle of the street.

The girl was wearing a grass-green uniform and carried an even larger shopping bag. Her hair was not the pale green tone that Aiz remembered but golden like her own.

It was the elven warrior who had shaken up the city with her introduction in the War Game—Lyu.

"…Good day to you."

"…And to you."

The two exchanged awkward pleasantries. It was clear at once that Lyu had only called out to Aiz because she'd seen her and not because there was anything in particular to discuss.

Aiz didn't really feel like she knew Lyu all that well. She understood she wasn't the most sociable person to begin with, but even so, the elf girl always seemed to avoid her whenever she came to the bar. If Aiz didn't know any better, she'd say it was almost as if the two knew each other from some long-ago time, and Lyu was trying to conceal that fact.

In any case, now that both had stopped, it would be strange if neither of them said anything further, so Aiz summoned all her limited vocabulary and subpar communication skills in an attempt to rekindle the conversation.

"…Have you been shopping?" she asked.

"Yes. I'm just picking up some things for the tavern," Lyu replied. "And yourself?"

"They changed the flavors…so I went round the Jyaga Maru Kun stalls…"

"…I see."

Unfortunately, both Aiz and Lyu were far cries from their respective associates Lefiya and Syr when it came to the power of self-expression. Neither had a great repertoire of conversation topics to draw upon, and, thus, another awkward silence lingered.

Nevertheless, the miniature self inside Aiz's mind drew her wrist across her brow and exhaled, as though a monumental task had just been achieved.

"Good-bye, then."

"Yes, good-bye…"

With that, both girls set off in opposite directions, but just as it seemed the bizarrely curt encounter was over...

"...Sword Princess!"

Lyu stopped and called out to her, as though finally cutting through the indecision in her heart.

Aiz turned back and tilted her head, awaiting the elf girl's next words.

"Would you mind...accompanying me for a while?" Lyu asked.

"There's something I really must apologize to you for."

Outside a roadside café, Aiz sat silently and stared into Lyu's sky-blue eyes. She hadn't the faintest idea what this could all be about.

"A few months ago," said Lyu, "on Daedalus Street, when the armed monsters were attacking, I tried to take you by surprise. I deeply apologize for assaulting you that day, no matter what my reasons were."

"...Huh?"

The elf's admission triggered a protracted silence. Lyu looked confused, and at length, Aiz's eyes widened.

"...You mean..." she said, "that elf I fought was you...?"

"Did you...not realize?"

"Well...you had a mask on."

"...I assumed a woman of your caliber would have realized as soon as you saw me in action during the War Game..."

Oh.

Aiz blithely stared off into space. Now that she mentioned it, the elven warrior she saw that day did conduct herself in a manner awfully similar to the masked adventurer who attacked her on Daedalus Street. In fact, they were exactly the same. A few levels apart, perhaps, but the basics of their style, tactics, techniques, and innate skill matched perfectly. Now that she saw it spelled out, why *hadn't* she noticed it before...?

But while the little girl inside her mind was putting on her judge wig, preparing to pass her sentence, Aiz frantically tried to appeal in her defense.

Of course, she had other things on her mind during the War Game, like Bell. Not to mention, Lyu's appearance came as such a shock in the first place that Aiz didn't have time, or rather the mental capacity, to put two and two together. It didn't mean she was stupid, just…overworked! Despite her fevered plea, however, the ruthless mini-Aiz handed down a verdict: "Guilty by virtue of being an airhead."

Okay…so…

In summary.

Lyu, the elf from the tavern, was in fact the infamous Gale Wind of *Astrea Familia* who had participated in the most recent War Game. Not only that, but she was also the masked adventurer who had assaulted Aiz on Daedalus Street…

Lyu began to grow concerned at Aiz's lack of outward reaction, but beneath the surface, the gears were turning. Suddenly, a question occurred to her.

"Have we…fought before? …In the past?"

A distant memory of an ancient meeting resurfaced in her mind.

"Before Daedalus Street…in the Age of Darkness…?"

"…Yes, we did. We crossed swords, and we also fought side by side to end a great threat."

So many years had passed since that first duel that Aiz could no longer remember what had possessed her young self to fight. All she could remember was a desperate desire to grow stronger, along with vague impressions of a mask, cloak, and wooden sword.

The second battle, however, she remembered well. For it was then and there, seven years prior, that Aiz fought together with the late warriors of *Astrea Familia* to bring an end to a devastating war.

She was not a member of her familia, like Finn. Nor was she a friend, like Bell. Yet Lyu was still a comrade, one with whom Aiz had shared the battlefield on many occasions, even if only for a short time.

"When I first met you seven years ago," said Lyu, "you were a child, causing grief for Lady Riveria...Perhaps it's rude of me to say, but you seemed spoiled. Over the years, though, I've watched as you came to the tavern, each time just a little taller, a little more grown-up. Honestly, I think it's amazing, the way you've matured..."

For the first time in the conversation, Lyu smiled.

Aiz had no family, but for that moment, she wondered if this was what it was like to have a loving big sister watching over her.

At the same time, she was a little embarrassed. She knew full well how troublesome she'd been as a child and didn't need to be reminded of it.

Aiz wondered why Lyu had never revealed any of this before, but she soon concluded that there had been no need. Gale Wind had always been on the Guild blacklist and a wanted woman besides. That she had come clean just now was pure chance, that was all. Lyu had happened to spot her on the street and decided there was no need to keep secrets any longer.

Aiz thought back to all their meetings across the past seven years. A strange feeling of destiny came over her, and she decided to ask nothing more.

"...You don't need to worry..." she said. "About Daedalus Street. I don't think anything of it."

"Seeing as you defeated me that day, I'm not sure how to feel about that..." Lyu replied. "But I suppose that means my apology has been accepted. With that out of the way, would you mind if I asked you something else?"

Aiz stared back blankly, and Lyu posed her question. It was an exceedingly simple and purehearted one.

"That night on Daedalus Street," she said, "I felt a vast gulf of power between us. What have you been doing these past five years while I was retired?"

A simple question from the former Gale Wind to the Sword Princess, a girl who kept running on, just like she had in their battles together.

Aiz wondered what Lyu could hope to gain from such a question, but looking into her sky-blue eyes, she concluded there was no deeper meaning. She was simply saying what she felt.

"I fought monsters..." Aiz answered. "...In the Dungeon...Lots and lots of them..."

After the Age of Darkness ended five years ago, Gale Wind vanished, with some even saying she'd died. Aiz, on the other hand, continued venturing into the Dungeon, to that crucible of monsters, where she hacked, cut, and killed them. Many floors. Many slaughters. Many wounds suffered in exchange.

And so in addition to her alias of War Princess, Aiz became known by another name: Monster Slayer.

For five years she did this, honing her blade and herself. Five long years of the same.

Aiz's dispassionate, almost coldhearted answer caused Lyu to fall silent. Eventually, Aiz opened her mouth and added something else.

"But," she said, "just as much as that...It's thanks to the other people in my familia...They've helped me out so much...Especially these past six months."

Aiz thought back to *Loki Familia*'s recent expedition where they managed to reach the fifty-first floor. It was only thanks to the likes of Riveria, Tiona, Tione, Finn, and Lefiya. Countless times they had helped her, protected her, and raised her to the heights she stood at now. Aiz believed that without question.

"Is that right...?" said Lyu, who smiled gently.

"What about you?"

"Hm?"

"You're a lot stronger than the Gale Wind I knew from back then...How did you manage that?"

Before she realized it, Aiz had opened her heart and asked the same question in return. As she awaited Lyu's answer, she stared at the elf girl with wide golden eyes and dazzling golden hair no less radiant than her own.

"I went on a journey," Lyu replied.

"'A journey'...?"

"Yes. I thought I could no longer stand for justice, but I found it impossible to remove it fully from my life. Instead, I pursued a false justice. But these days...I believe I've found myself a real one."

There was no way Aiz could fully understand the significance of Lyu's words.

What she could understand, instead, was that the smile Lyu wore at that exact moment was so much brighter than any to be found within her memories and that the elf girl's days of wandering, lost in a dark maze, were finally over.

Only those who had been with her through hardships and sorrows and seen the joys that lay beyond could perceive the gentle arc that traced Aiz's lips just then.

Two travelers exchanged a pleasant account of their journeys.

The wind passed between them and bound them together.

And then, after a long silence, Lyu's expression turned grave.

"...Sword Princess."

"...What is it?"

For the first time in their conversation so far, Lyu dropped her gaze to the table, and Aiz felt that the mood had changed somewhat and that something very unexpected was coming.

She stared in confusion, waiting patiently for Lyu to get the words out, until...

"What do you think of...of Bell?"

Aiz's eyes widened. At the same time, Lyu's whole face went scarlet.

I-I can't believe I actually asked that!! And I asked the person Bell idolizes! The one I've known since she was just a little girl, half my size!

Had one been positioned in her lap, facing up, one would be treated to a magnificent view of the elf's flushed features. Lyu squeezed her eyes shut, trying to forget all about the humiliating words she'd just uttered.

After a series of events resulted in her finding out who her beloved admired most, Lyu couldn't help but find out how he was seen in return, no matter how ill-spirited she thought it was. That wasn't to say that the entire conversation so far had been for this purpose, but since the opportunity had presented itself, Lyu couldn't let it pass her by. At least, this was the excuse Lyu had prepared in her mind even though nobody asked.

After finally averting a meltdown by shedding heat through her long ears, Lyu lifted her head. Aiz was still staring at her, wide-eyed. And, as if suddenly thinking, "Oh, you're serious," she began to give the matter careful thought. That was enough to make Lyu feel embarrassed all over again.

At excruciating length, Aiz parted her soft lips to speak.

"I think Bell's…" she said, "…a rabbit."

"A what?"

"Lady Hestia asked me the same thing. I think he's an adorable white rabbit…or something like that?"

Lyu wasn't sure how to react to that answer. Was she supposed to be relieved or stand up and bellow, "How dare you force me to make myself vulnerable for this!!"?

However, Aiz wasn't finished yet.

"But," she said, "I have been thinking about Bell…more often recently."

Ever since the goddess posed the very same question, Aiz had found her feelings changing with every new interaction with the boy.

In the incident with the Xenos, the pair nearly came to blows and made mistakes that neither of them could ever take back.

When the fate of the city hung in the balance, Aiz had nearly lost herself to the black flames, and it was the sound of one white bell that saved her.

In a fabricated world, he had said it wasn't wrong to try to meet her.

Why did he do that? How had he grown so strong? And why did he say those words?

More and more these days, Aiz found herself loosening her grip on her sword and staring up into the clear blue sky.

But when she did, it was not in sadness or anger.

For now, Aiz wore the smile not of the Sword Princess or the War Princess but of a little girl.

Seeing her smile, like a single white flower in a mountaintop breeze, and hearing the things in her heart, Lyu's sky-blue eyes widened.

"Why? What do you think of Bell?" Aiz asked in return.

"...M-me? I...er..."

Lyu was caught off guard and couldn't answer.

Her face and ears were bright red.

But she wasn't afraid.

No mountaintop flower was going to intimidate her into silence.

And so a proud elf made up her mind.

She opened her lips to speak, and then...

"Huh? Lyu and...Ms. Sword Princess?"

"What are you two up to?"

At that moment, a gray-haired girl and an amber-haired elf strolled by, catching the pair by surprise.

"Just small talk, that's all," said Lyu. "We just happened to run into each other. What about you? I don't often see you two together."

Syr smiled. "We just ran into each other as well," she said. "I just can't wait to learn more about Bell, so we're conducting a street interview!"

"Hey! Speak for yourself! I couldn't care less about that rotten human!"

"Oh, that's funny," said Aiz. "We were also just talking about Bell and what we thought of him."

"WHAAAAAAAAAT?!"

Just as Lefiya tried to steer the mood away, Aiz dropped a bombshell that ignited the air around this one café table all over again.

"Oh, wow, same as us, then! Well, since we're all here, why don't we have a little girl talk? The topic can be *Who Loves Bell Cranell the Most?* I think you'll find my obsession is a force to be reckoned with!"

"Syr, I don't think that's as laudable as you seem to think…"

"Are you all interested in Bell as well…?"

"N-not me, Ms. Aiz!! How could I ever care about such a stupid, ignorant…?!"

And so a couple more chairs were pulled up, and the table became a little more crowded.

The sun bathed the city in amber light.

A pair of winds, cold and gentle, swept the street.

And a gray head of hair tied it all together.

There, on a street corner where four roads met, the voices of four lively young girls echoed far and wide.

Afterword

This collection of short stories contains articles from *Sword Oratoria* Volumes 1–12, *Familia Chronicle* 1 and 2, as well as those spanning other media as of 2022. The only exceptions are the stories "And So the Girl Sets Off Running Once More," which was an unpublished work from *Sword Oratoria* Volume 10, and this last piece, "Four Paths of a Half Year," which was newly written for this volume.

This is my second collection of short stories, focusing on *Loki Familia* and the girls of the Benevolent Mistress.

It's a bit late to point this out, perhaps, but *man*, there are a lot of characters in this series. I mean, that's why there are all these spin-offs but still. There are so many that often, when I'm tasked with a short story, I find it difficult to pin down who to write about!

You might think, well, at least I'll never run out of ideas, but in fact, having so many choices makes it so much harder to write. Which characters should I include this time and how should they interact? With the only limit being my imagination, it just means I spend all that time wrestling with indecision instead. Maybe that's why there are so many short stories this time around.

As much as I'd like to include everyone, as soon as I try to put, say, four characters in a story designed for two to three pages of a paperback book, I end up with no space for anything to actually happen. I envisaged putting a small number of characters on a tiny boat together and watching as that boat either sailed off into the sunset or sprung a leak and capsized (in the case of a joke skit). I'm sure I'm only going to end up adding even more characters (*sigh*), so it's time to start thinking about who will ride that boat in the future.

With that out of the way, it's on to the acknowledgments.

I extend my deepest thanks to my editor and benevolent master Usami for putting up with all my whining at the last minute. I thank the artist nilitsu for all their beautiful illustrations. I especially love the cover image this time around, and I look forward to working with you again on the next volume, as imminent as it may be. A final thank-you goes out to everyone who worked on this book and everyone who picked it up. I express my deepest gratitude from the bottom of my heart.

It is currently May 2023, and next month will see the publication of *Orario Stories*, a collection of short stories included in the anime Blu-rays. I apologize for the pressure this places on everyone's wallets! Of course, you are free to engage with my work to whatever extent you desire, but if you can pick it up, I would very much appreciate it.

Thank you for reading this far, and until next time.

Fujino Omori